Pistols and Pedagogues

Pistols and Pedagogues

by FALLON EVANS

SHEED AND WARD - NEW YORK

For Jane, again.

Pistols and Pedagogues

Chapter 1

It was half a day's train trip from Chicago to the campus of Saint Felicitas and the journey was uneventful. Which means that I spent the whole time locked in the jakes. Of course, I would have offered to pay my fare if the conductor had discovered me. At the little town of Stratford I disembarked. The way to do this is to wait in the jakes until the last possible moment, then to walk down the aisle carrying your suitcase and peering about as though you were looking for an empty seat. The conductor whom you have avoided by your voluntary solitude will assume that you just got on until he sees you swing off just as the train starts to move. It is much simpler to accomplish this trick if you have a few stickers from the more expensive colleges stuck onto your suitcase because conductors are all intellectual snobs. Even though I'm entitled to several tony escutcheons, I can't use this easy device anymore. When people see me carrying a suitcase with *Chicago* or *Harvard* or *Catholic U.* stuck on they feel that I must have stolen the bag and are liable to call a copper.

I stand five feet three inches in twenty-eight dollar elevator shoes when I can afford them. At the time I swung off the train before the eyes of the indignant conductor I was wearing two pairs of heels nailed to my shoes. I stand only five foot two with the double heels. Rich or poor, I wear a raggedy red beard, but at the lower height my beard bristles in kind of a gesture to the world. It is the beard that makes college stickers seem inappropriate, whereas in fact, the beard is the offending part because I *am* a student.

I am what we call in the trade a professional student. I appealed to my father's better nature for years until I had nearly depleted his resources in tuition and book bills. After the war I signed on for the G.I. Bill, and for more than four years I lived on the monthly government check signed by Paul Banning, Disbursing Officer, who in time came to be rather a father image to me. Then I spent a year in Paris, boy is Paris wild, on a Guggenheim that I won on the strength of a small, erratic and erotic book of verse that I wheedled a friend of the moment into publishing. After that there were months during which the world and I eyed each other bleakly. It looked as though I were going to have to get a job, but a Fulbright dissipated that bad dream and woke me, as it were, to reality. Boy is Rome wild.

It was in Rome that I grew the raggedy red beard. Before the growth I was like a man without a country. I mean, the little *paesanos* ran after me to sell me fountain pens and the American tourists tried to speak to me in pidgin English. After the beard nobody spoke to me at all. Well, once a

Dominican priest — this was during the Holy Year — asked me very politely where Keats' tomb was, and I told him that Keats was buried in Vatican City because the priest was a nice guy who was probably looking for sermon material, and I figured what the hell, a sermon about John Keats' death-bed conversion might do a lot of good, say, at a mission in Deer Trail, Colorado.

Back at the U. in Chicago I was plundering a small grant offered by a private foundation whose only thought was scholarship and beating the tax racket. It was there that I first met Bartie Barstairs, who was responsible for my trip to Stratford and the campus of Saint Felicitas. The grant was small and I tried to eke out my beer budget by working in a poolroom on the Southside. Usually I found that I had to sell my textbooks before the term was over, and I came to know Bartie by constantly borrowing his books. He was in most of my classes and this worried me because he was obviously working rapidly toward the degree and my big problem was to take enough courses to keep the scholarship without taking the courses that would force me through the curriculum and so out into the real world. Once you get that Ph.D. it's almost impossible to keep on taking classes as steady work. And people have little patience with jerks who have finished all the requirements but haven't written the dissertation yet. The trick is to avoid taking a couple of required courses.

I found to my relief that Bartie's advisor had recommended all the wrong courses, so it was all right for me to take the same classes. Usually I avoid counselors because they only want to get you through the damn school, and because I am usually some ten or twelve years older than the advisor. Bartie finally changed advisors and found one who showed him how to zip through the doctoral program in record time. I knew the name of that guy but I never allowed Bartie to use it in my presence.

Some pretty queer ducks wind up on college faculties and it was clear from the beginning that Bartie was a chosen one. He spoke quietly, haunted Harper Library, dressed conservatively, and drank two beers every Saturday before retiring. It was destiny that he was going to become a college teacher. Knowing that he made it to six-thirty Mass at Mount Carmel every morning, that he never swore except with deliberation, I predicted accurately that he would wind up at a small Catholic college for girls, which is just what Saint Felicitas was.

I was still taking classes at Chicago when he was awarded the degree and was hired by Saint Felicitas. We corresponded sporadically. He would write asking for this or that book that I had borrowed from him. Bartie had always demanded the best in the scholarly line and his books were pretty valuable, so I always sent the book back to him, if I still had it. Many of them had been sold to pay debts of honor. He had one book in particular that I had hated to sell. It was a copy of *Beowulf* with a pencilled interlinear translation that had come straight down from a class of George Lyman Kittredge's at Harvard in nineteen-ought-five. One semester I borrowed that book from Bartie and then rented it out by the hour to the more backward students.

Every couple of months, then, I mailed a book to Bartie or wrote an explanation. My finances were pretty tight and the future dim when I took that train trip locked in the airless jakes. It hadn't been altogether a schoolboy lark. Bartie's letter hadn't included an advance.

Rumpledredskin:

Saint Felicitas sets aside a certain sum each year to invite a visiting lecturer to open up new worlds for us. Mortimer Adler declined to come, even for forty-five dollars and expenses. Or so I have heard. I have now sold them on the value of the Red Menace.

I told them that only the continuous prayers of the community could account for the fact that you are available next weekend, the feast of Saints Perpetua and Felicitas. Will you come for fifty dollars and no expense account?

I assume that the above is an academic question. Mary and I will put you up and put up with you during your visit. Mary is working out her first pregnancy now and probably won't speak to you but I am middling confident that she will smile upon you.

I have touted you to the administration as a world-wide authority on James Whitcomb Riley. Your speech on Friday next (for which, I remind you, you will be paid FIFTY DOLLARS) should contain extensive quotations from 'Li'l Orphant Annie' and should mention in passing that Saint Felicitas was gored by an enraged cow.

You will be a success. Come Thursday, stay until Monday. I want you to meet Jim Downey who is right out of *Lear*.

Bartie Barstairs

P.S. Hoosier psychologist?

7

I sent a collect wire to Bartie at Saint Felicitas college:

SHALL LECTURE ON RILEY'S BEST WORK
CRHYMES OF CHILDHOOD.

BARBAROSSA

Anyone who has spent as much time in literature classes as I have knows something about everybody who ever put pen to paper. Even old James Whitcomb Riley I knew something about even though American poetry wasn't my field. It's strange how an education can broaden your outlook and narrow it at the same time. For instance, I have spent hours on depth analysis of poems, sometimes bad poems too; but it had never occurred to me to try a depth analysis of a place. Stratford when first I saw it I took to be just what it looked to be on the surface: a little town with a college at one end and a few small manufacturing plants at the other, supermarkets and such in between, busy on Saturdays, sleepy on Sundays, then quiet but clean until the next Saturday.

There was a subdued bustle about the train platform; a few people arrived, though of course I hadn't seen them on the train. The redcaps piled luggage and mail bags onto their yellow wagons. This is just how large Stratford was: a bearded juvenile leaping off the evening milk train just as it left the station attracted no attention. The Stratfordians were blasé.

Three cabs were lined up, all in the shadow of the yellow brick station. I stuck my head into the window of the first taxi to ask how much a ride to Saint Felicitas College would cost. The driver, a thick-wristed goon in a greasy leather jacket, eyed me sullenly.

"I'm just going off duty," he said. The difference between cab drivers and train conductors should be plain; the cabbies have contempt for college students and for suitors of the hand of Mnemosyne, Mother of Muses.

"Well, there's something in it for you if you give me a ride there," I said, crawling into the back of his filthy cab.

Here again classy college stickers on my suitcase would have helped. As it was, I had to count on his knowledge of my destination coupled with what I hoped were previous bitter experiences with college types. For atmosphere I sang a few snatches of college songs. He didn't try to make conversation and so I felt pretty certain that the correct thought patterns had been established. I lolled in the back seat, but I was peering rather intently at the street signs.

Stratford was larger than I had thought. There was a "downtown" area running to shabby dress shops, office-supply stores and Walgreen Drugs. The residential sections were pleasant, with wide streets and overarching trees, the houses set well back, the lawns well-tended, the most of them recently raked of leaves. Just about the time that I first glimpsed the red brick campanile of Saint Felicitas, I saw Bartie Barstairs' street flash by. And just half a block beyond I saw the conveniently high hedge that I sought.

"Look out," I cried somewhat urgently, "I'm going to be sick." That was a mental reservation; it was true enough to predict an illness of the flesh. Sooner or later, I meant,

9

what with all the new viruses going about and with the hours that I keep. But the cabbie had me associated with Boola-Boola and those unfortunate experiences in his cab on prom nights. He slammed on the brakes with a jar and a curse. I threw open the door, leapt out with my suitcase, staggered a few steps to the hedge, then bent double and ran like a red fox.

I don't want to blame Bartie for not offering me an advance on that fifty dollar lecturing fee. I won't say for sure that I would have arrived in any other fashion even if I had had more than seventy-eight cents in my pocket. But I never did explain the details of my breathless arrival at his front door, for fear he would feel guilty.

Bartie greeted me with bated enthusiasm. As I had predicted, he had married just before his graduation. I had also predicted that he would owe money to Sears and Roebuck up until the time of his retirement. Now Mary was in her last months of pregnancy and she was enormous. They both were avoiding excitement. Bartie was a great believer in prenatal influence and, scholar that he was, he wanted quiet children who would wail only in muted tones and leave him alone to do his scholarly research. There was a microfilm viewer in a corner of the front room, a great metallic box with lights and spools and a large viewing screen that allowed Bartie to examine microfilm reproductions of Old English texts. They both referred to it as their TV because they were trying to condition themselves and the unborn child. They had a pathetic hope that the kid would think that all the other families had microfilm viewers in their front room too.

The room was quiet and shabby; it was a furnished house and Bartie and Mary had added only the microfilm viewer and a large, stark cross in the dining room. Both bits gave the apparent poverty a rather ennobling effect.

"Red," he cried at the door. "Come in, come in, come in."

I was inside by that time of course, and I had closed the door behind me in case that cabbie was cruising the neighborhood. "Mary!" he continued. "You must meet Mary. Mary, Red's here. Are you all right dear?"

Mary came in and we both said fine and how are you. She was a bit puff-eyed and, as I said, large with child, but she was a beauty. I don't mean underneath it all, or despite her pregnancy. No, she was beautiful in her pregnancy. She came into the room, dark-haired and rather waddling.

I'm not really self-conscious of my height, but I am aware of it and pregnant women have a tendency to overpower me. Almost anything oversized has this effect: the freshmen that come to Chicago U. these days, for instance. Years ago in a rush of misdirected patriotism the University gave up football and converted Stagg Stadium into a factory for atom bombs, so the really big boobs began going elsewhere for an education, to Minnesota and Notre Dame. Places like that. Even so I was an inch or two shorter than any of the arriving freshmen. For a little while there they admitted students in short pants, prodigies and such, and even *they* were taller than I was. Without the bristly red beard I look like a wizened juvenile; with the beard I still look like a juvenile, but a bearded juvenile. The beard makes people think that I'm trying to conceal something. And I am, of course. It's all that wizen.

Mary asked me about the train trip down and I gave her a moving description of the countryside, of the excitement of the train, of the people riding in my car. Almost right away Bartie recognized the description as a paraphrase of Thomas Wolfe's *Homeward Angel,* so I gave it up and admitted that I had taken a Pullman and had slept all the way to Stratford.

I think that Mary recognized this as a paraphrase of an old Baron Munchausen routine because she heaved herself to her feet and swayed out to the kitchen to fix me something to eat.

"I've invited Jim Downey over for later this evening," Bartie said after Mary had left the room. "I thought we could sit around and talk, and we might be able to give you some idea of the level you should lecture at tomorrow."

So that was the first time that I heard Jim Downey's name mentioned aloud. I never knew so much about any man, nor ever really knew so little, as I knew about him. I never saw him, never spoke to him; and yet my whole life was changed by him. And I damn near died still playing the juvenile lead because of him.

Later on, when things got sticky in Stratford, I tried to run a depth analysis of Bartie's letter to find out, if I could, why Bartie had mentioned Downey in the first place, but I seemed to have left that letter in Chicago. By then I had come to the point of looking for subtle and sinister meanings

12

in everything, even in the face of my friends and the shape of his letter. When first I heard the name, I rather ignored it; what I did attend to was the pleasant picture of a long evening of talk with Bartie, Mary, and some guy named Whatchamacallem.

"Well, if we're going to have a long night of talk," I said, "let me run out and get some beer." I said this because I had heard the rattle of beer cans in the kitchen, and had just glimpsed Mary opening a can at the sink.

Jim Downey never arrived.

Mary brought a cold turkey sandwich. "We can't eat the turkey tomorrow, and it will be spoiled by Saturday," she said graciously as she set the sandwich on its chipped plate by the arm of my chair.

I wolfed it down, took a long swallow of beer and wiped my beard on a napkin that turned out to be an antimacassar.

"Tell me about old Saint Felicitas," I said.

"I thought we would wait until Jim arrived before we started filling you in," Bartie said.

Mary walked to the door of the kitchen where she could see the kitchen clock. "He's late," she said. "Jim's never late."

"Well, tell me about him while we wait. What's he like?"

"He's nice but quiet," Bartie said.

"Awkward, too," Mary said with a short smile to her husband. "He makes me feel awkward."

"The truth is, Jim is ill at ease around women."

"What in the world is he doing at Saint Felicitas then?"

"Most of the time he is being ill at ease."

The idea intrigued me. I thought that a real woman-hater, a first-class misogynist, might enjoy teaching at a women's college, haranguing and bellowing and flunking students right and left. But I had never thought of a shy and retiring teacher living out his days and hours in an agony of embarrassment.

"Is he tongue-tied most of the time?"

Bartie nodded. "He has nothing to say most of the time. That's what I meant by *Lear;* like Cordelia, Downey has nothing to say."

Mary couldn't be restrained. "Oh, tell him, Bartie, tell him."

"Tell me what?" I asked.

"When he does speak, he makes embarrassing Freudian slips. It is sheerest courage that drives him back every day."

I threw myself back in the chair, waving my empty can. "More beer, Mary, more beer." She wandered toward the kitchen again and Bartie continued.

"It's a terribly awkward position and I admire his determination."

"Why doesn't he just get married and take off some of that pressure?"

"He's not the type. Anyway where would he meet a girl?"

I thought about that one. It was true; professors just didn't marry their students. I have heard of such marriages, but I couldn't remember one instance in my long and I might even say unparalleled career as a student. Members of the faculty have no place in the life of the undergraduate student, except as a thing to be handled with care and used in its proper place, like a toothbrush glass.

Mary shambled back with fresh beer. "I called Jim's

house just now but there was no answer. I guess he's on the way over."

"What do the girls think of him?" I asked.

"They're fond of him in a way. They treasure his slips of the tongue. Some seem to have been locker room jokes for months."

"Do they have locker rooms at Saint Felicitas?"

"Darned if I know. Mary, do they have locker rooms at girls' schools?"

"What's a locker room?"

Bartie turned back to me. "No," he said, "that was just an expression. Most of the girls board at school, but go home on the week ends. That's why they have lectures on Fridays, then when the girls go home and rich Daddy says, 'What did you learn at school?' they only have to remember back to Friday afternoon to tell him something."

Mary wobbled aimlessly about the room as Bartie spoke. Time and again she pulled back the curtain from the front window to peer into the darkened street. I thought several times to ask her if she saw a taxi out there, but I held my peace.

"He's never late," she said finally. "Do you think something could have happened?"

Bartie looked distressed. "You shouldn't allow yourself to dwell on such thoughts, Mary. Remember the baby."

She smiled wanly. "All right, dear. You tell Red how Jim once told us how much cheaper it is to buy day-old bread." She gave him a peck on the cheek, brought me one more can of beer and oscillated to the back of the house.

"It isn't like him at all, but I suppose that something could

15

have come up." He looked at me for an embarrassed moment. "I suppose that we had better talk about your lecture."

"Do they really want a speech on J. W. Riley?"

"Oh yes, it's all been publicized on campus. This is, after all, Indiana, and he is the Hoosier Poet."

"I think I'll give them the old psychoanalytic jazz about reversion to infantile state and return to the womb, now that you have suggested it to me."

"Oh no, have pity on the nuns who run the college. Remember that none of the students have probably ever heard of James Whitcomb Riley; they were all brought up on television — Captain Video and his space gang. The nuns remember him, though; he's part of the memory of their Indiana childhood. 'The frost is on the pumpkin' and all that. Just be nice about the old guy; use your lovely phrases of vague praise, accept the check gracefully and keep your head high."

Twice during the course of our talk Bartie stepped into the kitchen to check the time and to call Downey's home. There was no answer. When the beer seemed to be gone, the night well into morning, we parted, he to the bedroom, I to stretch out on the frayed and springy sofa.

I don't know what time the telephone rang. I had been fully asleep, I know. Instinct simply took over when the telephone bell rang. Without pausing to remember that I was a guest in a strange house, I staggered to my feet, groped to the kitchen and in the dark located the telephone by touch and sound.

"Hallo?"

It was a girl's voice, harsh with strain but obviously young. "Is Jim Downey there?"

"Nah." But even as I uttered that monosyllable I heard the click and the steady hum of the telephone. She had rung off. I stumbled back to the sofa. I didn't check the time.

Chapter 2

THE NEXT MORNING was like so many mornings worse than you could think possible the night before. I was awakened early by the milkman who rattled an inordinate number of bottles against the front door. It was Mary who drank all the milk and I felt a rising tide of resentment against all pregnant women and overstuffed sofas. I wriggled around to extract a spring from the small of my back, but by then the sun was shining brightly into the shabby room. The harsh light illumined the poverty, exhibited coldly the cheap veneer of the ugly furniture. I realized with a pang how magnanimous had been their gesture of all those beer cans. And I felt resentful toward them both. I thought briefly of bouncing out of bed — not difficult to do with that old sofa — and preparing their breakfast. But I compromised by wrapping the blanket about me and curling on the floor. That way I wouldn't be any less stiff than if I had stayed on the sofa and they would feel compassion for me when they came out to prepare my breakfast.

Breakfast, when it did come, was a pretty sullen affair. Mary was being sick in the bathroom all the time that I brooded over my coffee.

Bartie kept saying, "I *know* that isn't good for the child." I finally did get into the bathroom but not until after Bartie had shaved. First I examined their medicine chest pretty thoroughly. There was no aspirin, but I took two Midol tablets and began to feel better. The shaving soap was inferior; I only shave a small area but I like the best. Bartie's after-shave lotion was expensive, obviously a Christmas gift that he was trying to stretch out until next Christmas. I used it liberally on the arm pits as a punishment for Bartie because there wasn't enough hot water to take a shower. I passed by Mary's calcium pills but took several of her vitamins to compensate for the breakfast, and then we were ready to leave for school. Bartie kissed Mary; Mary kissed Bartie. I repacked my bag. I didn't know that I would be moving out that day so I didn't think to pick up some additional razor blades or vitamin pills. I suppose it wouldn't have made any difference as things turned out.

It was a brisk fifteen-minute walk to school on sidewalks deep with fallen leaves. We spoke little. Bartie was apparently preparing the day's lectures, ordering facts and quotations in his mind. I had begun to brood on the wisdom of my trip. I was worried about what was happening in Chicago at the poolroom. If things were busy and business brisk the owner might be forced to the discovery that he was smart enough to rack up the poolballs all by himself, and then I would be out of a job. On the other hand, if things were slack the owner might have time to go over the cash-received accounts, and that, too, might have a terminal effect on my employ.

Saint Felicitas College rose before us, all red brick and browning ivy vines. There were four or five buildings of the ancient American Catholic mold called Irish Gothic. The most prominent features were the red brick, the wavy glass windows and the iron fire escapes. The land sloped away from us to the left as we entered the wrought-iron arch that marked the entrance to the college grounds. Through the autumnal leaves of the college trees I could make out the slate grey of a large lake. Students in bulky sweaters, plaid skirts and knee-length knitted stockings hurried between the ancient buildings. Here and there were nuns in fluttering black habits, their starched coifs the only touch of white in the landscape.

I breathed deeply and easily of the Indiana air; here on a college campus I felt at home. I knew that I could, with no further instructions, find my way to the classrooms, to the controller's office, to the office of the Dean. Blindfolded and spun thrice around, I could still walk directly away from the building that housed the offices of the student advisors. Chimes sounded across the crisp and pleasant air: a quarter to the hour. There would be time for a smoke before the next class.

Purposefully as a bee across the browning lawns of the main quadrangle a nun hurried toward us.

"Doctor Barstairs," she called when she was within hailing distance.

20

"Good morning, Sister Mary Ransom," Bartie replied. "May I present our guest lecturer for today, uh, Red Withers."

"Arid Withers?" she replied, eyeing me coolly. "What a strange baptismal name. Was your father a Christian?"

"Yes, Sister. He was Catholic." Now, years and years of experience as an altar boy were shown in that brief reply. I was still cranky and I was affronted by her tone and I wanted to make a stinging reply, but I could no more speak to a nun without saying "Sister," and saying it with proper respect, too, than I could bless myself with my left hand.

"I'm so glad that I encountered you before class," she continued, turning to Bartie. "As a matter of fact, I have been lying in wait for you. I prayed to Saint Felicitas, her feast day is today, you know, I said a little prayer that Mister Withers would be with you."

I felt a sudden kinship for Saint Felicitas. She, after all, had been gored by an enraged cow and I by a sofa spring. And now she had brought me right to the feet of Sister Mary Ransom.

"I'm delighted to be on the campus of Saint Felicitas College on the feast day of your patron," I said. I overdid it a bit and my voice bore a hearty note of false unction. Sister accepted the letter and not the spirit of my speech. At least she nodded and continued to address me through Bartie.

"Mr. Downey didn't appear at his early morning class and we fear that he won't be here in time for his next class. I wonder, Doctor Barstairs, if your friend would lecture to our students in Mr. Downey's class during this next period."

I listened to her speech intently because she was, after all, speaking about me. I can assure you that it was no question she put to Bartie. I was expected to report to Downey's class and hold the students' attention for fifty full minutes.

Bartie and I nodded vigorously at the conclusion of her proposal. He had probably been dreading my attendance at his lectures as much as I had. I think we had both experimented with the idea of my remaining with Mary until my lecture time, but the experiments had been brief and silent. He feared for his child; I for my peace of mind.

Now Bartie had an additional worry, the missing Jim Downey. "Jim has never missed a class. Even if he were desperately ill he would come to class. Last year he had a temperature of a hundred and three and he taught two classes that day." He was hurrying me toward the Academic Building, but paused to stare in the direction of the lake. "Jim lives in a cottage on the other side of the lake. The school leases it to bachelor professors. I suppose they must have called there by this time."

"Maybe he has a hang-over and is embarrassed to appear." It was the first of my many, many speculations on Jim Downey's disappearance. I offered it then with no real conviction and during the next few days of furious speculation I never returned seriously to the idea. Already I knew *that* much about Jim Downey; he was neither intemperate nor irresponsible.

Through the ancient doors of the Academic Building Bartie hurried me, down the dark corridor, a left turn and we stopped before an opened door.

22

"This is Jim's class. Think you can manage?"

"No doubt, no doubt. Will I see you after class?"

"Come to the Administration Building; we'll have a cup of coffee in the faculty office." Bartie turned and started away.

"Oh, Bartie?" He turned impatiently. "What course is this?"

He shook his head. "Ask the girls." And turning, he sprinted toward his own nine o'clock class.

The room was of medium size, student chairs were ranged in irregular rows before a somewhat battered desk. There I took my seat, glared at the surprised girls and folded my hands. They fell to a respectful silence.

"Do you begin class with a prayer?"

They nodded.

"What do you pray for?"

"Wisdom," said a girl in the front row.

"Patience," said one in the back. I fixed her with my eye.

"That custom will be honored in the breach this morning. What is your name?"

"Betty."

"Well, Elizabeth, do you recall the subject of this course?"

"It's Shakespeare, sir."

"Do not call me sir; you may call me 'Sister' if you wish. And what play are you studying?"

"*Julius Caesar*," they chirruped in a throaty chorus. I was on safe ground; *Julius Caesar* was a shoo-in for me.

"I presume that you all read *Julius Caesar* while still in high school. You were then too young to perceive its beauty. That play is assigned for high school reading only because

23

there are no dirty words in it — although Portia does pronounce the word *thigh*." Several of the students began to
take notes.

Fate was clearly toying with me. Already, and unwittingly, I was enmeshed in the life of Jim Downey, and my
first act was to lecture on the problem of discerning between
appearance and reality. What man in fact or history was
more confounded by the disjunction between appearances
and reality than Brutus? Unless it was myself, Adrian
Withers. I spoke at length (I had fifty minutes to fill) on
how Brutus had watched Caesar thrice refuse the Roman
crown only to conclude that Caesar wanted to be crowned.
Had I listened as attentively as the quiet students I would
not have made the error of confounding appearances with
the true nature of things.

Immersed in the topic, I was startled when Sister Mary
Ransom appeared at the door.

"Excuse me, Mister Withers, but would you call roll?"

"Surely," I said, and throwing back my head called, "Roll!"
It was a cheap trick and I admit it. It won the students to
my side at the expense of the sister. She smiled tightly,
pulled a roll book from some dark recess of her habit and
proceeded to call off the names of my listeners. All seemed
to be in order; one student was absent but accounted for in
the college infirmary. Betty informed me after class that the
missing student was a grind suffering from a richly deserved
and long overdue case of mononucleosis.

The class ended without further interruption; I chatted
with the girls for a moment, then was led to the Administration Building and Bartie's promised coffee.

24

"Well, the mystery has been solved," he said as I entered the dark and narrow office. "Jim Downey has run off with one of our students, Linda Brusick."

"You gave me altogether the wrong impression of that boy."

"You're not as surprised as I am. About Jim, I mean. I should have guessed it about Linda; she was about our prettiest student and she was, well, discontented with classes of late. Of course, she was an art major and it's hard to tell when they are with us and when they're not."

I sipped the black and grainy coffee. "Did they leave incriminating evidence?"

"Well, they both dropped out of sight last night. That's what the roll call was all about. Linda didn't report for bed check last night. She seems to have disappeared with Downey at just about the time he was supposed to be arriving at our place."

"He surely comes up in my estimation."

"He should. Linda is not only our prettiest student, she's the richest. Her father is Thumbs Brusick and he's supposed to have a slot machine empire in Chicago."

"Slot machines!"

"Oh, yeah," Bartie affected a casual attitude. "Quite a few of the girls are from, well, prominent families. This is a quiet college that affords, among other things, a refuge from publicity."

I put down the nasty coffee. "Do you mean to tell me that if she hadn't run off with Downey, she would be telling Thumbs Brusick all about James Whitcomb Riley tomorrow morning?"

Brusick I knew by reputation. Several months of each year, when the heat was off in Chicago, his mobsters carted three or more quarter slot machines into the back room of the poolhall. The machines would remain there, getting a brisk play for three weeks or a month, then they would be hauled away and we would know that the heat was on again.

"I wonder if Thumbs will find a place for his new son-in-law in the organization?"

"I doubt it," said Bartie. "They say that he's furious. I heard that he was on his way down here. Listen, can you entertain yourself here until lecture time? I have two more classes."

"I'll make a few notes for the lecture."

And I did. Nevertheless, I came down with the quivers at the last minute, just before the lecture. The trembles were partly the result of plain stage fright, partly the pangs of guilt. Something in me rebelled at earning money, even though I argued that it wasn't exactly honest money. After all, I knew practically nothing about old Riley. Still, the quivers came on and lasted until I stepped before the microphone in the crowded auditorium. Then I realized that I had left the notes on the desk in Bartie's office. They weren't very good anyway. I cleared my throat noisily, the loudspeakers whistled, the girls in the front rows clapped their hands to their ears and cringed in their seats.

The lecture was not a success. The microphone functioned improperly, the lectern was too high for me to be seen when I stood behind it. And, of course, the whole student body knew by that time that Linda Brusick had eloped with Jim Downey. The news was sensational. College campuses are

26

all closed little worlds, and the two leading figures of this world had committed a romantic and unthinkable act.

Only once did I command the total attention of the assembly, and that was during the moving rendition I gave of "The Congo."

"Mumbo Jumbo GAWD of the CONG oh, BOOOMlay, BOOOMlay, BOOOMlay, BOOOOOOM!" I shrieked with what I hoped were appropriate gestures. I realized almost at once that "The Congo" was written by Vachel Lindsay and not by James Whitcomb Riley, but I was creating an effect and it was effect that I was seeking at the moment.

The applause was mild and even that was cut short when an elderly nun, one who obviously bore authority on her shoulders, stepped to the microphone. Instantly the auditorium was still.

"My dear girls," she began venomously, "you are all no doubt aware of the events of the past day. You are all, too, doubtless aware of Saint Felicitas's reputation for discretion. We are not a publicity-seeking institution. We might even be said to go to great lengths to avoid publicity. Of any kind. If any of you mention this event to family or friend before the news is released by the proper authorities, which is in this instance myself and Linda's father, Mister Brusick — the girl who commits that indiscretion may not return to this college." She paused ominously. "Are there any questions? If not, the assembly is dismissed."

Backstage the same elderly nun offered me the fifty dollar check. "I was not aware that dear Mr. Riley had written 'The Congo.'"

"It's one of the lesser known facts, Sister. He also wrote one called 'General William E. Booth Is Ejected From Heaven.'"

"Indeed? The sentiment of the latter seems a happy one. I wonder, Mr. Withers, if we could prevail upon you to do one favor?" She still held on to one corner of the check as she spoke, so I inclined my head in assent. "We would like to know if Mister Downey left any clue as to his whereabouts or contemplated destination. Linda seems only to have taken a few of her things in one suitcase, which would indicate that she planned to return. We would like to know if Mister Downey has removed all his possessions. Or if perhaps he left a note. In view of the circumstances, and considering the fact that his house is rented from the college, we feel that we are entitled to search the premises. It would, perhaps, be unseemly for one of the nuns, however, and we wondered if you would examine his rooms?"

I was nodding and bobbing like a madman by then, but she still clutched a corner of the check.

"Mister Downey lived in the former caretaker's home on the other shore of our lake, only a pleasant ten-minute walk from here. Would you be to kind as to report your findings to Sister Mary Ransom?"

Snap! The check was mine. I turned smartly on my four heels, strode out of the auditorium across the campus and through the wrought-iron gates. I intended only to find a bank, to cash the check, and have a drink. But then I thought: Oh well, I might as well do what she asked. There is a certain fascination in prowling through other people's homes. I turned back toward the campus, the lake and the caretaker's cottage.

It was a small house and the grounds were untended. The path that led around the lake ended at the kitchen door. The front door faced onto a brambly patch of rank and withered grasses; that door was apparently never used. Within there were three rooms; these had been designated by Downey as kitchen, bedroom, and study. All seemed serene within, if somewhat sterile. The kitchen was tidy, a few pans piled on the back of the stove, one chair pushed under the table where he obviously ate. The variety and number of canned goods in the cupboard indicated that he cooked for himself.

The study was somewhat more cluttered. Books on the shelves leaned to right and left and it seemed clear that they had been much consulted. They were mostly textbooks and common reference manuals. Nothing of much value, worse luck. On the desk were piled ungraded examination papers, a back issue of *The American Scholar,* pencils, paper clips, an egg-shaped stone that served as paper weight, several books of matches and a date book.

I sat down at the desk chair, mate to the straight-backed chair in the kitchen, and read through the date book. Downey had recorded mostly college events: the days on which special seminars met, appointments with students, special assemblies at school. There was no mention of the meeting at Bartie's house the night before, but my lecture was entered and firmly underlined. He seemed to have been undergoing rather extensive reconstruction on his teeth for there were numerous dental appointments entered and scratched out. There was an appointment entered for the following week end and not lined out yet. Glancing back I noticed that all of the dental appointments were on week ends and I realized what a thoughtful lecturer Jim Downey was. I myself had once attended a lecture delivered by a scholar who came to the podium straight from his dentist's office. His mouth was completely anaesthetized, and he spoke and looked exactly like Buster Keaton.

All of the annotations in the date book seemed clear and patent; none seemed to refer to liaisons with Linda or to secret sessions of passionate planning. Would Downey have entered such things in his date book? I rather thought that he was the type who would put down a reminder to himself to be sure to attend such trysts, but of course I didn't know the man. And the fact was that he had not recorded a reminder of our intended soiree at Bartie Barstair's home.

There was the other possibility that Downey and Linda Brusick had discovered each other only the day before and that fire had blazed between them. They had spurted home, packed a few essentials like nighties and mouth washes and had fled into the night. The thing to check was how careful had been the packing.

The bedroom seemed to be as neat and orderly as the other two rooms. The bed was made, a narrow bed, I noted. His clothes were neatly hung in the closet, jackets on the right, then slacks hanging straight from metallic grips, shirts and sweaters to the left of these. On the far right of the closet hung his overcoat, raincoat and windbreaker. I slipped off my jacket and tried on a brown-and-white hound's tooth sportscoat. It fit quite nicely; it was three or four inches too long but most of my coats were. There was nothing in the pockets of that jacket. I slipped it off to rehang it and noted that there were only two empty hangers — only two places within the arrangement into which I could reintroduce the jacket I held in my hand. It would seem that Downey had taken only one coat, presumably the one he wore on his back.

The single gap in the row of shoes on the floor of the closet told the same tale: only one pair missing. I wonder what I would have concluded if three shoes had been missing? As it was, the conclusion seemed inescapable. Downey hadn't packed a thing.

I turned to the bathroom; if Downey had left his razor behind that would confirm the evidence of the closet. I opened the medicine chest. The razor was there all right, but it wasn't the razor that riveted my attention. The bottom shelf was cleared of bottles and tubes to make place for a string-necked sack of chamois cloth.

I carried the sack to the bedroom, untied the string and shook the contents out onto the bed. Even my limited experience told me that what I saw was a narcotics kit: several grey-looking pills, two folded paper envelopes, a blackened spoon, a book of matches, and a hypodermic syringe.

Gingerly I fingered the syringe as I thought out the process: the little envelope carefully unfolded and its contents shaken into the spoon, a match applied to the bottom of the spoon, then the liquid sucked up into the syringe, the needle in the arm. . . . Shouldn't there be something more? Would he cleanse the place of the injection by swabbing it first with alcohol? Did he enlarge the vein by binding his upper arm with rubber tubing?

Once more I returned to the medicine chest, but it seemed perfectly innocuous now that the chamois bag had been removed. There was a bottle of rubbing alcohol and cotton swabs, there were bottles of antiseptic and mouth wash and iodine and bromides. All things that a fastidious and perhaps hypochondriacal young professor might naturally possess.

Back in the bedroom I stared down at the kit. I was involved with Jim Downey a good deal deeper than I wished to be. In the first place I was reluctant to reveal my knowledge of the narcotics equipment. The mingled love and tolerance that showed in the eyes of Bartie Barstairs and his wife when they spoke of Downey was so evident, even when they were laughing at him, that I was less than willing to speak out about my find. I couldn't quite picture myself reporting back to the great stone face in the medieval coif that Downey has left in such a hurry he had even forgotten his heroin. No, that was out.

I was under no obligation to tell Downey's friend, nor to tell his employer. How I stood with the legal authorities I was not sure. It struck me then that the best thing to do was to destroy the evidence and to forget as much as I could of Jim Downey and his problems. Within twenty-four hours, I said, I would be back in Chicago. Within forty-eight hours I would remember nothing of Downey except for the few Freudian slips which I would retell at beer parties. "Thou shalt see me at Philippi," echoed in my ears for just a moment but I dismissed it for what it was, an inner echo from my class on *Julius Caesar*. I thought then, as I do in part believe now (for I learn from books and not from experience), that man can escape his nemesis.

I flushed away the evidence of the dope; thus I disposed of the powder and the paper envelopes. I poured what jewelry I found on top of the dresser into the chamois bag: cuff links, tiepins, collar clasps, and one paper clip. I dropped the bag into the top drawer among the handkerchiefs and socks fresh from the laundry. There it looked innocent and natural. The spoon I dropped behind the stove where it might never be found. I dropped the matches on the desk. I noticed that they were not of the same kind as those already strewn among the books and papers on the desk. Those atop the desk were imprinted *St. Felicitas* and had probably been purchased at the college book-store. The matches from the chamois bag were of the type distributed at drug counters. "Thank you, call again," was their message.

To dispose of the hypodermic syringe took more time and more thought. Finally I found a paper sack of empty cans outside the kitchen door. I broke the syringe on the kitchen table top, smashing the glass into splinters with the skillet from the back of the stove. The needle and the broken glass I scooped into the triangular hole in the top of an empty tomato juice can. Carrying the can outside I squatted on the path halfway between the cottage and the lake, and poured handfuls of dirt into the little hole. When the can seemed more than half full, I carried it to the edge of the lake and hurled it far out. As it broke the still surface I realized that I had done something irrevocable. For good or bad I could

33

not undo the act, nor could I with impunity reveal to anyone what I had done. I hoped that I had washed my hands of the whole business.

Sister Mary Ransom waited for me on the steps of the Administration Building.

"No clues, Sister. No notes. No indication of their destination."

"Well, thank you, Mister Withers, for your kindness. Does it seem to you that he left hurriedly?"

"Well, there's no evidence of haste. Everything seems to be in its place. I suspect that he took only the clothes on his back."

"It will be awkward for him when he returns for his belongings. His contract with Saint Felicitas College is, naturally, terminated. I'm sure he won't be a welcome figure on campus. He has put the administration in a difficult position; not the least of our worries is the problem of acquiring a teacher to fill out his contract. . . . I suppose you couldn't be persuaded, Mr. Withers?"

In the evening dusk it struck me with the light of reason that my affair with the Foundation would be ending with a bitter lovers' quarrel at the end of the semester. My job at the poolhall was at best chancy. And I found myself wringing her white hand in agreement. For a month or more, even until the end of the current semester, I would be receiving double pay, my check from the Foundation and Downey's check from Saint Felicitas.

"Oh, there are a few problems," I lied. "I have a number of commitments in Chicago. Lecture engagements and such."

34

"Perhaps we can partially compensate for your losses," she offered hesitantly.

"And then my apartment is leased for the season. . . ."

"Our budget is a limited one. I'm afraid that we can't help you there. . . . Of course, you're welcome to stay at the cottage. Mr. Downey's lease was coterminal with his contract; I'm sure he understood that as well as we do. We always make a point of stressing that when we lease the cottage. The lease is a formality after all, a dollar a semester."

"I'll put seventy-eight cents down now and the rest when I've cashed your check."

"No need, Mr. Withers. Perhaps we should step to my office; there I can show you the schedule of classes."

"Perhaps tomorrow, Sister, or Monday morning bright and early. I really would like to get to a bank before they close."

I trotted all the way to Bartie's house, the dried leaves crackling under my feet. There I breathlessly explained my position. Bartie assured me that the banks did remain open until six o'clock on Friday evenings, but the banks were in the business district in the heart of Stratford. No, he owned no car. No, he couldn't think how I might get to a bank before closing time. I trotted again, back to the street and the corner where I had jettisoned myself from the taxi. That street was obviously the main artery from the campus to the heart of town.

Time was precious to me now; I had less than fifteen minutes before the banks closed. It is not an easy thing (I had learned long before) for a bearded man to hitch a ride just at dusk. I hurried in the direction of town, and within

half a block I found the car that I wanted. It was unlocked
and parked near the corner. Quickly I switched on the headlights of the parked car, as quickly I stooped to unscrew the
air valve from the rear left wheel. When the tire was quite
flat I straightened up, turned with an angry and exasperated
shrug of my shoulders and flagged down an approaching car.
The very first car stopped. I hopped in beside the driver.

"Got a flat tire, buddy?"

"Yes, damn it. You going to town?"

"Yeh."

"Will you drop me off at the filling station across from the
bank. I know that guy."

He idled the engine as he thought. "There's no service
station across from the bank. Which bank do you mean?"

"Oh well, the station just this side. You know. . . ."

"Oh, the Standard station."

"That's right. I know the guy."

"Okay, but you left your lights on, buddy."

"To hell with them, let's go."

I got to the bank just before they pulled the shades on
the front door. Minutes later I was wealthy. Wealthy, I
thought as I stood on the sidewalk in the gloaming looking
for the friendly flicker of a tavern's neon. *And* I was gain-
fully employed. At long, long last Brutus was an honorable
man.

There seemed to be no bars on the main street of Stratford. On a parallel street, back of the bank and two blocks to
the left, I found a bar. As I stepped inside I realized that I
had somehow crossed the tracks. The bar was a tough one. I

speak as a man of some authority, for I have seen men as well as slot machines carried out of that poolroom on the Southside of Chicago. The light was dim inside, most of it coming from electric lights within animated signs advertising different beer brands. The four or five men at the bar paid no attention to me as I clambered up on a tall stool.

I pushed a ten dollar bill, crisp and green, before the bar tender. "Do you have any imported beers?" I was resolved to reward myself handsomely for having earned money.

He eyed me narrowly without taking the cigarette from his mouth. He was big.

"Yeah, they're all imported from Milwaukee."

"Well, open one for me, and see what your writers will have."

He removed the cigarette, stubbed it out with deliberation in the ashtray before me, then slowly turned to the cooler. He removed a bottle of beer and studied the label. I think he was trying to antagonize me, but he might have been trying to identify the brand by the pictured trademark. At least I know that he wasn't reading the label; that was a skill beyond him. In time he brought the bottled beer and a glass. He didn't offer to pour.

"Will you bring me some dimes with the change? I want to play the machine."

"We got no slot machines in this town," he said when he returned with the change.

"Well, I feel pretty lucky; I think I'll try the telephone then."

I slipped off the stool; the imitation leather seat was sticky and my trousers peeled noisily away from it. In the filthy telephone booth at the back of the bar I looked up Bartie's number in a tattered telephone book. Mary answered the phone.

"Hullo."

"Hullo, Mary, this is Red. I am wealthy beyond the dreams of avarice."

"Bart wants to talk to you."

"I know, but wait a minute." I realized that she had simply walked off to get Bartie without bothering to answer.

"Hallo, Red?" It was Bartie.

"Hello, Bartie."

"Sister Mary Ransom has been trying to get in touch with you. Did you really offer to take over Downey's classes?"

"Yes." I wished that I had drunk the beer before coming to the telephone.

"Don't you think that Jim Downey will come back?"

"Sister Ransom suggested that he wouldn't be welcome."

"I suppose you're right. I hadn't thought about that. Well, listen, there's a class tonight."

"What?" It was a terrible blow to a man of my wealth and inclinations. I saw that a steady job would be onerous beyond standing. "A class at night? What kind of a trade school do you run?"

"Well, it's adult education, a service to the community kind of thing. I had it last semester."

"Would you take it again tonight?"

"I'd like to, Red, but I don't even know what course it is."

"Neither do I."

"And I'd hate to leave Mary alone."

"Send her down here."

"I'm sorry, Red. I thought that you wanted the job. I mean, I didn't press it on you. *I* didn't even know until Ransom started calling on the phone this evening."

"Never mind, never mind. I'll take it. Where does it meet and when?"

"It meets in the Administration Building at eight."

"Okay. If Sister Mary Ransom calls again, put her mind at ease. One more thing, is there a legitimate means of transportation in this town?"

"A bus runs right down the main drag, along Western and stops at the main gates of the college."

"Thanks, I'll see you tomorrow sometime."

"Won't you want your bag tonight?"

"No, Bartie, thanks." I knew that Jim Downey had left behind all that I would need for the night.

I finished the beer as rapidly as I could, shook my head "no" when the bartender feinted toward the beer cooler. He looked at me contemptuously when it was clear that I would buy only one drink.

"Did you have any luck on the phone?" he asked as I started for the front door.

"Phone?" I paused in the doorway. "Phone? I thought that booth was the urinal."

Stratford was quiet with the quiet of a Friday evening lull as I stood at the bus stop before the closed bank. Thrifty souls who had taken advantage of the before-six o'clock prices were all gathered in the movie houses; the devil-may-cares who were willing to pay a quarter more to see the same film a half an hour later had not yet left their homes. A few cars passed me. Some of the young fellows driving alone in shiny cars were undoubtedly headed for Saint Felicitas and a Friday night date. I didn't try to flag any of them down. Youth is an age of conformity. None of them, I knew, would dare drive up before his girl, open the door of the car and let a scruffy, red-bearded creature hobble out to make room for her. I felt scruffy then, and I had begun to hobble a bit since one of the heels on my right shoe had become loose.

But the bus stop was a pleasant place to be. Even in the business district of Stratford trees grew; they rose from earth squares set in the concrete sidewalks, and arched over the sidewalk and over the street so that the light from the street lamps was pleasantly diffused. Here most of the buildings were dark, but a block away I could see the bright lights of a supermarket. Two blocks in the other direction the two movie houses faced each other across the broad street: the theater section. With a rumble and a squoosh the bus pulled up before me. I was the only passenger.

Perhaps a dozen people stood in the corridor before the door of the only lighted classroom in the Administration Building. Several of them leaned against the No Smoking sign and puffed meditatively on their cigarettes. That meant, of course, that there were no nuns about.

"What class is this?" I asked.

"It's Mr. Downey's class."

I turned away from that inept and foolish informant and walked into the classroom. There were perhaps another half a dozen people scattered about the room. I knew where I belonged; my new status demanded that I stand behind the lectern, but the habit of years is hard to break. Every instinct in my body cried out to direct me to the rear of the room and an inconspicuous seat by the window. It was difficult to stand before the class, my back to the blackboard. In the seat that I would have occupied had I been still a student there sat a familiar figure. It wasn't someone I knew and yet he was familiar. I crossed the room to stand before him.

"What's the name of this course?"

"It's called Great Books of the Western World," he said.

"This is the right class then." After all, I wanted to save face. "And the Great Book you are studying now is. . . ."

"Dante, *The Divine Comedy*." I was home safe again. Only one more question and I would be ready to lecture.

"How long does the class last?"

"An hour and fifteen minutes. Are you going to join the class?" He was a bland little man; his pale complexion was a bit exaggerated by the classroom lights and the grey suit he wore. There was nothing distinguished about him or distinctive, and yet I had a nagging feeling that we had met before.

"I'm the new teacher. Mr. Downey won't be with us anymore."

He accepted that announcement without any signs of shock or outrage, saying simply, "Oh?"

"Listen, have we met before?"

"I think so. Didn't you go to Chicago U.?"

That was it. The bland little man still sitting as he spoke

41

to me, looking up at me with a steady, veiled gaze, was a semi-pro. He was one of that group who take night classes all their long and uneventful lives. Unlike the professional student, they choose only non-credit courses and usually courses that are known to be easy. It isn't intellectual stimulus they seek apparently so much as it is the feeling of belonging to collegiate life. Some of them take the same classes year after year, following a regular cycle that allows them to repeat the same class with a different teacher every third year. That way they can use the same textbooks and can be reasonably confident of understanding what's going on in the class. Or at least of knowing what's going to happen next. Others of this group will identify with one professor and will take every course he offers until in the regular succession of classes and years they come to know all his jokes, all his quirks, all his family problems.

I couldn't remember much about the bland gentleman, not even whether we had shared a class. I wondered briefly if I had borrowed a book from him; he showed no animosity toward me.

As a matter of fact he showed little curiosity. He neither supplied his own name nor asked for mine.

I toddled to the front of the room, cleared my throat and stood quietly rocking on my loose heel until the students had filed into the room and taken their seats.

"My name is Mr. Withers. I am now on sabbatical leave from the Saint Felicitas Home for Aged Sisters and I have been asked to fill in for Mr. Downey for the remainder of the semester. The lecture for this evening is entitled, 'The Influence of Dante Alighieri on James Whitcomb Riley.'"

The lecture was all right; again my recitation of "The Congo" was well received.

But it was exhausting work. At the three-quarter mark I feared that I had already revealed everything that I had ever learned. I realized for the first time how demanding the pedagogical profession was; either one had to prepare one's lectures or call upon profound depths. Had I been a married soul I would simply have filled in the remainder of the period with anecdotes of my private life. As it was, I was called upon to stir deep and muddy depths of my memory. When the bell rang I stopped in mid-sentence.

"Thank you and good evening. Last one out turn off the lights and clean the erasers." I waved discreetly in the direction of my Chicago acquaintance — it would give him status in the class — and left ahead of the students.

Following the path around the lake to the cottage, I realized how tired and hungry I was. Among Downey's canned goods I found some beans, which I ate cold from the can, and several pieces of oldish bread. I undressed quickly, found a pair of freshly laundered pajamas, a great luxury for me even though they were several sizes too large, switched out the light and tumbled into the narrow bed. I fell asleep almost as I laid my head upon the pillow.

Chapter 3

THE SUDDEN LIGHT awoke me, not the noise that must have preceded it. For a moment I didn't know where I was; I couldn't remember where I had gone to bed. Nor did I know how long I had slept. If awareness had not almost immediately flooded back I might have wandered out into the world a saintly mendicant, completely disengaged from the things of this life.

But a voice cried, "Here he is," and I knew they were talking about me.

"I knew my daughter wouldn't run away with a teacher. Get him up." It was a rough and rasping voice out of *De Contemptu Mundi*, a voice nearly barren of illusions. I didn't see the speaker, or at least I saw only his back, for he had turned to join the others in the study. I wasn't left alone. At the wall by the light switch stood an ugly gnome: a small, dark, tough man; although clad decently in black even to his shirt and tie, he seemed somehow obscene. The

44

product of what slums was he? Perhaps it was congenital evil he represented, or incestuous passion.

"You heard him, get up."

Groggily I plucked the blanket back and swung my feet over the edge of the bed. My toes didn't quite touch the floor, but the pajama cuffs did.

"Hey there, Thumbs? This guy's a cripple. You know, like a Geek?"

My head was clearing, although I still squinted painfully because of the bright overhead light. I rolled up the trouser cuffs of Downey's pajamas, slipped my feet into my unlaced shoes, picked up my coat and twisted into it as I stumbled toward the study. It was Thumbs Brusick, come to Saint Felicitas to look for his daughter, and I for my part intended only a summit conference. I wanted no small talk with a gnome. He stood unmoving, his hand still on the light switch until I had almost reached the door, then he shifted his weight heavily and put out a restraining arm.

"Wait a minute, you. Thumbs! You ready for him?"

"Can he walk?" Thumbs called.

"Yah, he's got like braces on his feet."

I could see Thumbs Brusick from where I stood. He sat in the straight chair before the desk; he didn't choose to glance over his shoulder.

"Send him in."

There were two others in the room with Thumbs Brusick; any one of them might have been a featured player in a Class C horror picture. Or perhaps they looked like gargoyles. I don't know, all of these comparisons came to me

45

later. At the time I was barely able to see, blinded as I was by sleep and shock. I had only to explain to Linda's father that I was not the Jim Downey who had eloped with his fair daughter and all would be well; but I had trouble articulating, for my lips were dry, my throat drier. I approached the middle of the room, put forth my right hand and emitted a thick noise of welcome. Brusick glanced over his shoulder, then looked back to the desk.

"Geez," he said.

I wasn't looking my best but his contempt seemed a bit extreme. There were three of his men standing behind me now and they were apparently accustomed to being addressed without being looked at, for Brusick continued aloud and they listened attentively.

"The money for tuition doesn't count, but you guys know what I pay for Linda's education. I can afford the best for her and I paid for the best, too."

One of the thugs shoved me from behind to show his agreement with Thumbs' sentiment. Thumbs turned then to face us but not to admonish the myrmidon who had shoved me.

"I told them in Chicago, didn't I? And I told the good Sisters, 'Linda wouldn't run off with no teacher. She's got too much pride,' I said. And I hadn't even seen this guy yet. Geez."

I was shoved from behind again; this time with enough force to push me off balance. I half turned.

"Cut that out."

The gnome slapped me.

It was terrible. Of all the things that happened to me afterwards, none was worse than that. It was a brutal, malicious, and perfectly conscious destruction of my personal dignity. It had been, at that time, nearly a year since I had touched or been touched by another person except in the most formal or most fleeting and impersonal fashion. I mean a true and human touch of flesh against flesh. In that year I had shaken hands with people; several times my hand had brushed another as I handed an ivory cue ball across the counter of the poolroom, but there had been no intimacy there. But flesh against flesh — man at the most basal and elemental level forcing his will upon another by the sheer fact of his material weight — that had been alien to me for nearly a year. A revolver is not the true equalizer of men, nor is his animal nature the lowest common denominator of man; it is weight, the ultimate obedience to blind gravity that equalizes the differences in men and makes the gnome as great as the troll, the thug as grand as the student.

My world was toppled; in a sense more real than literal, I was brought to my knees before these stupid men.

I turned from my tormentor to face Thumbs Brusick, who now stood. He was taller than I, but who isn't? His face was round and smooth, the eyes small, even tiny, but black and vital. There was a quality of robust good health about him that could not be attributed to his way of life but rather, I suspected, to his peasant ancestors from the Middle East. He bellied up to me, his eyes darting about my face, his unprotected stomach a mocking challenge; even as he approached I sensed that the three thugs had ringed me from behind. I leapt nimbly to my left, landed on the balls of my feet and whirled. My feet spread wide apart, my knees bent, I crouched forward from the waist waving my arms in the classic pose of the Japanese wrestler.

"All right, you sods," I shrieked, "Come on! Do you think a guy of my size hasn't learned something about jujitsu? I'll throw you in each other's fat faces. Come on, if you're so brave. I'll kill you with a chop." I clawed dramatically at the air before me until the gnome stepped up and drove a smashing fist into my face, just to the left of my nose. He didn't feint; he didn't pause. Something in my posture had told him that I knew nothing about jujitsu. I staggered back and slumped against the wall.

"Good work, Tabor; that's the way to get some of the tuition money back. Is he still frisky?"

"Nah, Thumbs."

With such reassurance Thumbs dismissed me from his mind. I pulled myself to a sitting position and wiped the blood from my nose on the tail of Downey's pajama jacket.

"I told you Linda wouldn't elope." Thumbs was addressing his goons. "Ever since she was so high I've been promising her a big wedding in the Cathedral, you remember? Anyway we've got the proof now. I don't know where that creep in the corner was yesterday, but he didn't run away with my Linda. So now the question is, where is she? And haven't I been telling you all along?"

The three lieutenants nodded their heads to the degree that their thick necks would allow.

"Paddy Grogan picked her up, that's where she is. For months he's been trying to meet me to talk business about cutting up the Southside, but he knows that I won't talk with scum like him. So he's kidnapped my daughter; he's going to hold her until I talk with him."

"You wouldn't think he had the guts."

"He needs action. Anyway, I know this: he wouldn't dare hurt a hair of her head. He knows I'd kill him myself."

"Right."

"And we'd wipe out his whole organization."

"What will we do, Thumbs?"

My own little gnome, the one they called Tabor, answered first. "Kill."

"Not until we get Linda back. First we gotta get Linda back and then Pow! to Grogan."

They deployed preparatory to leaving and only then remembered me.

"What'll we do with the teach?"

They watched as I pushed myself erect and stood with my back to the wall.

"Maybe he knows where Linda is," said one of the goons. "Ask him where he was yesterday when they nabbed her. How come he was missing too?"

"Okay, Weisenheimer, where were you?"

"I'm not even Downey." There seemed to be a high and fluting quality about my voice. "I'm not even Downey and I never laid eyes on your daughter. Downey's gone. He's gone away."

"Whose house is this?"

"Well, it's his house, of course. Or rather, it *was* his house. It used to be his house."

"But he moved out?"

"That's right."

"Whose stuff is this, then?" Brusick swept the desk top clear; books, papers, pens and matches scattered across the room.

"It's all his, I just moved in."

The five of us looked about the room like visitors to the Sistine Chapel; we peered and craned our necks, taking in details of the study. In the soft glow of the lamps it did look to be a cozy room, one much cherished.

"He just moved out and left all his stuff, and you moved in?"

Thumbs strode into the bedroom and the five of us, Tabor shoving me, crowded in behind him. He stood at the door of the closet nearly filled with neatly hung clothes.

"And all these threads, they're not yours either?"

"That's right. The clothes all belong to Downey, he. . . ."

"But you live here and he doesn't?"

"Let me explain. . . ."

"Geez."

"Wait a minute, Thumbs." One of the body guards stepped forward to observe me closely in the harsh overhead light of the bedroom. I dabbed at my beard now incrusted with dried blood from my nosebleed. "Sure, I know this guy. Sure, that beard and all." He turned to Thumbs. "This guy came into the bar this evening where I was waiting for you. I was sitting at the stool in front, looking out the window for your car, and this guy came in. He ordered one beer, looked the place over real quick, made a telephone call to somebody about what he had seen there; then he beat it.

50

"First he peed in the telephone, then he beat it."

"Hey, I know him too." It was Tabor. "Don't you work racking balls in a poolroom in Chicago?"

I nodded. "That's right. I'm not Downey, you see."

But Tabor turned from me. "He ain't Downey. I've seen him for years. He racks balls in one of those places in the sixties. It's the territory that Grogan wants."

"I seem to be in the kidnapping business too," Thumbs said. "Tabor, you keep your eye on him; the rest of us better shake the place down. See what we can find."

They were very thorough. They emptied drawers, threw clothing on the floor, pulled apart the bed. From the study a steady succession of thumps marked Thumbs' progress as he systematically shook open the books from the bookcase and threw them on the floor. They were creating a shambles and once I started to protest, but Tabor looked so obviously keen on hitting me again that I held my peace.

In time the noise ceased and Tabor shoved me to the doorway, where I could see the utter havoc that Thumbs Brusick and his thugs had created. Even then an overturned bottle was dribbling its inky contents across the desk and onto the floor. Not a book remained on the shelves, not a drawer was left in place. Thumbs looked with some perplexity at the chaos. "Well, the place is clean."

"What did you expect to find?" Tabor asked.

"I don't know. I don't know. Something about Linda."

"Look, Thumbs, I don't mean to say anything, but are you sure that Paddy Grogan got Linda? I mean, don't it figure that he knows what you plan to do when you get Linda back?"

"It's Grogan all right. He needs the action and he's taking the chance. He doesn't think I'd dare to drop him, not if Linda is okay when she gets back. But I will."

"Are you sure she didn't just run away?"

"The teach is still here, isn't he?" He jerked his thumb at me. It was a flattened thumb, I noticed, the nail almost gone.

"I was thinking in the room there," Tabor persisted. "Just because I saw this guy in Chicago don't prove that he ain't not Downey." I struggled with the treble negative, but Thumbs seemed to understand.

"You Downey?" he barked.

"No, I'm Red Withers."

"He might just be saying that," Tabor growled.

"Of course, I'm saying it: I'm Red Withers. I'll say it again. . . ."

Tabor hit me. It was a staggering blow to the ear that made my head ring and my knees knock. I turned to Tabor, tears of anger and humiliation in my eyes, but I tried to keep my voice level.

"Don't ever hit me like that again."

Pow!

He didn't; he hit me right in the middle of the forehead. I sagged to my knees.

"Wait a minute, Tabor," Thumbs said. "If this *is* Grogan's boy, he'll want to see him in good condition before he turns Linda back to me."

Tabor, his short legs spread, stood over me. "Go on, Thumbs, you can't give this guy back after what he heard; you said you were going to get Grogan good."

Brusick turned away from us and walked to the desk; he righted the chair and slumped in it, suddenly an old man.

"Sometimes I hate this business. Why can't I just run a few slots and be done with it? Who's hurt by a slot machine? Some sucker loses a nickel or a dime; maybe he blows a dollar in the machine, so does his wife go hungry? He gets his kicks; is it any worse than a penny arcade at Lakeside?"

The thugs shook their heads and made sympathetic noises.

"So what's your name, boy, and it better be Downey."

I tried my best to look sincere. "My name's Withers, but I'm taking Downey's place here." As soon as I said that I realized that I should have lied. I should have insisted that I was Downey. I could have admitted it with a rueful grin and a boyish shrug of my shoulders. And that would have been the end of my adventure with Thumbs Brusick. What I said was, "I'm a substitute teacher. I just arrived here last night and I'm taking Downey's classes at the college here. Really."

"That sounds reasonable. You got identification?"

I reached for my wallet and realized how scantily dressed I was in Downey's rolled up pajamas and my own jacket.

"In my wallet on the dresser," I said. "There's a check made out to me for fifty bucks. Adrian Withers."

Tabor gave me a parting shove on the shoulder and disappeared into the bedroom. In a moment he was back with my wallet.

"There's no check here."

"That's right. That's right." I nodded my head like a mad man. "I cashed the check this evening. I forgot that I had

cashed the check. That's why I was in the bar this evening."
I woggled around on my knees to appeal to the bodyguard
who had reported seeing me in the bar.

"Did he cash a check?" Thumbs asked.

"I tole you, he oney peed in the telephone."

There was a silence, broken only by a nervous giggle that
seemed to come from me. "Well, there's fifty dollars in the
wallet, less the price of a beer and one phone call and a bus
ride."

Tabor shook his head at Thumbs. "There ain't any money
in the wallet."

I mark my birth as a discreet creature from the next
moment, for just as I cried, "You thief!" Tabor slapped me
across the face with the leather wallet. It stung too, even
though it wasn't the jarring kind of a blow that he had already dealt. But, curiously, I smelled the wallet as it hit my
face: an odd odor so distant and yet so familiar. It smelled of
worn leather, of much use, and startling to me, it smelled of
myself. Our own odor is something that we each carry with
us, an invisible nimbus. I am rarely aware of the odors ema-
nating from another — sexy perfumes excluded, of course —
and I had never really smelled myself until that moment
when clad in Jim Downey's laundered pajamas, surrounded
by Downey's things, attacked by strange and violent men, I
suddenly caught the astringent odor of worn leather and Red
Withers. And I realized with sudden objectivity my own
position. I was in trouble. If Thumbs Brusick decided that I
was a henchman of Grogan I might find myself settling
silently into the muddy bottom of the college lake beside the

54

broken hypodermic syringe and weighted tomato juice can.

"There's other identification, of course," I said, my voice calm at last and quaverless. Truth, I felt instinctively, must at last assert Herself and save Her devoted wooer. "There's other identification in the wallet."

But there wasn't. How I cursed a world that takes cognizance only of numbers. Tabor found a library card and several dry-cleaning tickets for clothes that I couldn't afford to bail out of the laundry; there were numerous pawn tickets, a holy picture. . . .

"Har!" Tabor guffawed. "Here's one that says, 'In case of accident notify a Catholic priest.' Thumbs, will you give the padre a ring?"

In all the cards and tickets I was identified only by number.

"Now I remember," I said. "I'm Jim Downey."

Tabor started for me but Thumbs halted him with a wave of his hand. "Not here. We can't let him get back to Grogan, not after what he heard. We're going to have to have never seen this boy before."

Well, the splendor of the human body! The sheer delight in life that resides in the littlest of us. Even as I tried to comprehend the full import of Thumbs Brusick's words, my multi-heeled feet gathered themselves beneath me. By the time that I understood that Thumbs planned irrevocable damage to me, I was in full flight. Tabor lunged for me; the body-guards leapt for me. Thumbs shot up from his chair. There was a tangle of clutching arms at the kitchen door. I slipped through, wrenched at the kitchen table and spun it across the doorway. In the same instant I threw open the kitchen door and sped into the dark.

I bounded down the path twenty yards, turned abruptly and crashed into the autumnal underbrush. The noise of my flight appalled me, and I turned again to make for the damp vegetation by the edge of the lake. Even there my feet in the unlaced shoes seemed to pound thunderously on the damp grass. Would my pursuers shoot?

It was a dark night and they would pause for a moment at the doorway to accustom their eyes to the dark. I tore along the edge of the lake wondering where I should go. The safest route would have led me to the girls' dormitory. There, I knew, was one empty bed. For just a moment I held the vision of myself in askew pajamas and unlaced shoes pounding my way into the dormitory at Saint Felicitas.

I have been all my life long, and evidence to the contrary notwithstanding, an admirer of law and order. Neither the dormitory nor the dubious sanctuary of the college chapel would save me from the wrath of Thumbs Brusick. The stalwarts of the Stratford police would. Thither I directed my staggering steps.

Through the iron gates of the college I sped and down the leafy street that led to town. I was alternately trotting and staggering as I passed Bartie Barstairs' street. Halfway to town I was reeling in a drunken walk; had the police of Stratford been half what I hoped, I would have been picked up long before on a charge of drunk and disorderly conduct or indecent exposure.

But all was silent save for the sound of my feet in the fallen leaves. The houses were shut and locked for the night; the street lamps glimmered dimly through heavy trees. No automobiles crawled the streets. It would have been about my luck of a day ago — middling poor — to encounter my deceived taxi driver. But my luck had plummeted to an unprecedented low and I saw no one until I came to the quiet business district of Stratford and saw ahead of me the globular lights of the police station.

It was a brick building, unswept and silent. From the front door a narrow corridor, lighted dimly, led to the back of the building. The blurred crackle of a police radio came from the back of the building and I started down the corridor, supporting myself along the stained wall. A door opened suddenly and a policeman stepped into the corridor buckling his belt. He stopped in surprise at the sight of me. I was clutching at the stitch in my side, gasping for breath, and rather bugging my eyes at him.

"Hey, here he is now," the policeman called over his shoulder. He stepped back and beckoned me into the room with a click of his meaty fingers. I was unable to talk, but nodded and stumbled after him.

It was an office; filing cabinets piled with mimeographed releases stood along two walls. In the center of the room stood a battered desk of fumed oak, its top littered with newspapers and paper cups. In the swivel chair behind the desk sat the man who later identified himself as Chief of Detectives George Salter. He was a rugged man, a stone figure of a man with a face ineptly chiseled from granite. His hair, black and straight, was slicked back from a narrow forehead. He was a man you would trust implicitly or distrust completely; nothing about him spoke of compromise. He waited until I had stumbled to a chair before his desk and had crumbled into it. I held up one hand weakly, trying to indicate that he should sit patiently there until I had my wind back.

"I was just sending Dan here out to pick you up," he said. "We received two calls about you from out near the College Heights District. . . . Did you run all the way here?"

I nodded weakly.

"Good time. But why did you come here?"

I patted my chest, nodded my head, held up one hand, swallowed dryly. He watched my pantomime indifferently.

"Why did you come here?" he repeated. "You know I'm going to have to charge you with voyeurism."

My throat was still fiery but that charge seemed to win back my wind. "WHAAAT?" I croaked.

"You know what a voyeur is?"

"Sure, it's. . . ."

"Never mind, I know what it is. The fact is that only police and you creeps know what the word means. You sick creeps read up on it, all of you. To the average, clean-living, *normal* man the word means nothing. He talks about Peeping Toms. If you know what voyeurism is, it means you've been reading up on it, probably Krafft-Ebing, and in my book you're guilty."

He leaned forward and examined my face. I examined *his* face; the eyes were narrow and hard too, the nose somewhat shapeless.

"Did someone catch you peeping a window?" he asked.

58

I felt my forehead where his glance directed me and encountered the goose egg that Tabor had raised with his last blow. It was sensitive, and under my sympathetic probing it felt enormous.

"I've been hurt and pushed around and threatened, and that gnome stole my fifty dollars," I started in a rush. "And I came to you or they would have killed me."

"Wait a minute before you start making countercharges. Voyeurism isn't such a serious charge; you'll get psychiatric help if you'll take it."

"I don't want a head shrinker, I want protection. Those guys wanted to kill me tonight."

Deliberately he pushed the newspapers from his desk and withdrew from a top drawer a thick pad of yellow paper. This he put in the center of his desk and deliberately laid a pencil atop that.

"My name is George Salter; I'm Chief of Detectives, Stratford Police. Now I'll listen to what you have to say if you want to go through with it, but I'm going to take notes on it, and you better be telling the truth. Okay?" He poised the pencil.

"Could I have a drink of water?" Salter nodded and the heavy-set policeman brought me a minute paper cup filled with warm water. His beefy hand made the cup appear ridiculously small. "Okay, thanks. I'll tell the truth all right. There were about a dozen guys and they all hit me. . . ."

"We'll start at the beginning," Salter observed dryly, and he noted the date and the time at the top of the page. It was three o'clock Saturday morning.

"Your name?"

"Adrian Withers."

"Age?"

"About thirty."

"Age?"

"Just thirty."

"Male. White. Caucasian," he pronounced as he wrote. "Permanent address?"

"I've just been hired by Saint Felicitas College and I'm going to live there, that is, I was there tonight for the first time."

"Occupation?"

"Professor." For the first time of many the pencil paused. Salter glared at me from under his tiny forehead. "You're not under oath, Withers, but for the last time I'm warning you to tell the truth."

I pulled my jacket tighter about Downey's pajamas and tried to look professorial.

"I'm a professor. I'm taking Jim Downey's place; he's the guy who ran off with the girl from Saint Felicitas."

"What's that? Dan, did you hear about this?" Salter hurled the last question in a rasping voice.

The patrolman moved forward from his place by the water cooler. "What do you mean?"

"Did you hear that Downey ran off with a girl from the college?"

"Says who?"

"Well, it's true that there's a difference of opinion. Thumbs Brusick doesn't believe it."

"Who? Is Thumbs Brusick in Stratford? Are you sure?"

I touched the enormous bump on my forehead again. "Well, this isn't the mark of Zorro."

Chief of Detectives Salter arose to address himself to the patrolman.

"Why didn't I know about this? Am I to think that you forgot to tell me or that you didn't even know that Thumbs Brusick was in town?"

"I can't keep track of every two-bit thug that passes through town," the patrolman replied with a shrug.

"Thumbs is not a two-bit thug. He practically owns the Southside of Chicago."

"Oh, that guy?"

"Yes, *that* guy. Better I should fire you all and hire Peeping Toms if I want to know what goes on." He turned back to me.

"How do you know that Thumbs really is in town?"

"I thought he was the one who called you about me. I mean, when I arrived here you were ready to look for me, and. . . . Didn't he call you?"

"Old Lady Fish called me; she spends all night looking for prowlers and she saw you running down the street. She reports something like that several times a week and I would have ignored it only there was another call, too. Mrs. Barstairs called in to report a naked man running down Western. She's pregnant and can't sleep and she was out on her porch when she saw you go by."

"Really!? Mary Barstairs reported me?"

Salter studied me for a moment. "You know her, huh?"

"Well, really, I know her husband."

"Dan," he called to the policeman, "What do you make of this boffer?"

"Ah, he was making out with the old lady when this Barstairs walks in. This guy leaps out the window, but not before Barstairs sees him, so she calls us to befuddle her husband. 'Did you see somebody run down the stairs as you came in?' she asks him." Dan affected a falsetto when he mimicked Mary. "'I think I did too. I think I'll just call the officers.'"

I was stunned; after all, I had come to them to seek protection. And I had been accused of voyeurism and lechery. It was preposterous and yet it seemed to me that there was something calculating about their charges. They seemed to be baiting me, and yet Salter took the precaution to write down both charges and my reply to them. My reply didn't take long to transcribe. It was a one syllable word.

"Never mind that, you," Salter said. "Tell me where you learned about Thumbs Brusick."

I related as honestly as I could all that had happened to me that evening. I was continually stirred to an honest endeavor because Salter took down all that I said. I was thus careful to tell the exact number of thugs that Brusick had with him; I fought down the temptation to depict Tabor as a giant because I wanted Salter to have a description so accurate that he could arrest Tabor on sight. I concluded with my flight to the police station.

He leaned back in his chair. With an effort he extracted a crumpled pack of cigarettes from his trouser pocket, shook out one bent cigarette and lit it. He picked up the pencil again and with it shoved the pack perhaps a half inch in my direction. "Want a smoke?"

"No. I think those things stunted my growth. I'd like another drink of water, though."

The policeman, Dan, again lumbered to the darkened corner of the room and brought back a small, damp paper cup half-filled with warm water. There was hardly enough water to lay the dust on my teeth; it was my ration for the night, however.

Salter drew heavily on his cigarette. "What hotel is Brusick going to stay at?"

"He said the *best*. I don't know."

"What do you think happened to Downey?"

"I don't know. I never even met the guy."

"Well, why do you think the nuns out to Saint Felicitas didn't report him missing?"

"They think that he eloped with Linda Brusick. I told you that."

"Do you think that he did?"

"Sure. I don't know. What else could have happened? Oh well, I suppose that he could have just walked away. I don't know."

"And one more thing, Withers. What do you want me to do?"

"What do I want you to do?" I twisted in the chair, irritated by Salter's calm, or apparent calm. "I want you to arrest those guys. Get that Tabor particularly. Look what he did to me." I pointed to my bumpy noggin. "You ought to know what to get them for: assault and battery, intent to kill, breaking and entering. . . . What do you mean, what do *I* want you to do?"

"All right, now wait a minute. Calm down. Try to imagine for a minute what would happen to me if I were to walk into whatever hotel Brusick is at now and try to arrest him on a charge of assault."

That really wasn't a hard picture to imagine. In a flash I could see Salter stretched out on the floor of the hotel corridor. "Tabor would clobber you."

"Yah. Well, maybe. Anyway, *if* what you say is true, it's pretty obvious that I can't walk in there alone. So let's suppose that I get Dan to round up a bunch of his boys and we break into the place and pick them all up. That would look good, wouldn't it. Twenty-three members of the force — the total force except for those on sick leave — employed in one raid to get a guy for alleged assault. And not, according to your story, for assault with a deadly weapon. Just plain assault."

"If you're worried about getting a bad press, I apologize for having suggested that you have anything to do with criminals." It made me furious, his calmness and reluctance to move. We were about even then, because it seemed pretty clear that I irritated him. Still, he spoke quietly.

"Well, would you like to spend the night with us?"

"You mean, all you can do is offer me police protection in the cooler?"

Salter stood and walked slowly to the window. "It's almost morning anyway." Then he turned, nodding to the towering Dan, and fixed me with his pig-eyed glance. "I'm going to hold you on suspicion of the murder of James Downey."

Chapter 4

Lake Leman lies by Chillon's walls:
A thousand feet in depth below
Its massy waters meet and flow;
                              J. W. Riley

AT STRATFORD the jail occupies the second floor of the police building. Whereas the first floor had seemed shabby and cluttered, the second floor was antiseptic and empty. There was a drunk tank at one end of the building; this was for the common sort of drunks and the night that I spent in the Stratford jail there were none of these. Between the tank and the check-in stand there were a number of cells for murderers, thieves, embezzlers, pederasts, and poor innocents like myself. These, too, were empty until I arrived. It was apparently a quiet night in Stratford.

I protested loudly that I could not be booked on a charge of murder. I was amazed and delighted with the stamina and vigor with which I protested Salter's charge, for I had caught only a few hours' sleep that night and the night before that I had spent on Barstairs' beastly sofa. Whether my protestations were of avail or not, I do not know; I don't think that I was booked on a murder rap. I think that Dan simply caught me by the scruff and marched me up the stairs and into a cell.

Salter had looked stolidly toward me.

"Do I look like a murderer?"

"No," he replied quietly. "If I could tell a murderer on sight my job as a detective would be no-end eased. Look at it from my point of view. If I were to let you walk out of here this morning nobody in Stratford would understand. Least of all my boss. Frankly, you look too simple to have committed a crime, but that will be a problem for the prosecuting attorney to worry about.

"All I know is that this Downey guy disappeared and you moved smoothly into his place, his job, his house, and from what I gather from your appearance, into his pajamas. Somehow you were able to convince the Sisters at Saint Felicitas that all was on the up and up. But then, worried about what we might learn, you came in here with a cock-and-bull story designed to throw suspicion on a Chicago syndicate."

"Cockandbullstory! Where do you think that I got this bump on my head?"

"A guy like you, anyplace. Remember I already have ground for charges of Peeping Tomism."

"I can disprove that charge and you know it. I can get you for false arrest. I can . . ."

"Shuddup," said Dan and that reminded me that, however

66

Brusick's mob and Salter's police force might be opposed, they were aligned in a desire to smack out at me.

"Look," I began patiently, "Downey disappeared from Stratford with Linda Brusick on Thursday. I arrived in town on Friday . . . no, Thursday evening."

"Can you prove it?"

"Prove that I arrived here on Thursday? Sure, just call Bartie Barstairs, out near College Heights."

"What can he prove?"

"He will swear that I arrived at his house just at dusk on Thursday evening."

"And you think that this will prove that you weren't in town, in Stratford, for hours or days before?"

"Well. . . ." As a matter of fact, I saw his point.

"What about a fare? Have you a train ticket or a receipt of some kind that shows you took the Thursday train?"

"No. . . ."

"No? You mean, you threw it away?"

"I didn't buy a ticket, but listen, the conductor will probably remember me getting off the train here at Stratford."

"Let me tell you what I think. I think that you arrived here on Wednesday, destroyed the ticket, killed Downey on Thursday, then met the Chicago train at the Stratford station on Thursday evening, made a commotion — maybe you ran through the train, right? And tried to make such a spectacle of yourself that the conductor who didn't notice you at all the day before would remember you as the guy who created the fuss on Thursday."

"Listen, I couldn't *kill* anybody."

"Everybody says that," said Dan.

"Could a guy like you," Salter asked, "get a job at a college, at a place like Saint Felicitas, say? Could you get a job there if you wanted one, could you get it unless someone quit or something?"

"You're stacking the cards. Of course, I couldn't get a job unless someone quit. But that doesn't mean. . . ."

"Dan! Take him away."

And so I was frog-marched out of the cluttered office, up the stairs and into a cell. Dan slammed the door that had stood open and it closed with a note of metallic finality. Without another word he turned and plodded out through the check-out room. I looked wildly around my cell for a tin cup; in the Cagney tradition I intended to rattle it against the bars and cry, "Screw!" after Dan. But the cell held only a small basin, a lidless toilet and a metal cot; the thin mattress had a surplus army blanket folded at the foot. I sat on the cot, tucked my feet up and wrapped the blanket around me. The letters US on the blanket struck me as an ironical comment on my solitude.

It seemed perfectly clear to me that Jim Downey and Linda Brusick had run off together. That was the theory of the administration at Saint Felicitas and they should be in a position to know. If only Thumbs Brusick would admit to that, I would be safe. He had only to acknowledge that his daughter had shown execrable taste — as had her mother before her — and all would be well for me. And if Chief of Detectives Salter would accept the same obvious solution to the dual disappearance, I would be freed from his foul

68

oubliette. As a matter of fact, the cell seemed quite hygienic, but rather tastelessly gotten up.

For the time being I was safe, and sooner or later Downey and Linda would be discovered rollicking in some disreputable motel. If Saint Felicitas would issue a statement, or if Salter sent out a bulletin, they would be discovered that much sooner. As dawn began to show through the barred window of the cell I stretched out on the cot. My last thought was a vague but irritating one. I remembered, just before oblivion, the narcotics kit I had found in Downey's cottage.

Salter woke me when he unlocked the cell door. It was full morning, the sun high overhead, but it was chilly in the cell. I sat up but Salter didn't enter the cell.

"Get up, gargle, and come on down to the check-out room. I've got some coffee." He turned away and I tottered sleepily behind him, draping the blanket over my shoulders. There were paper cups of coffee and several large, sugary doughnuts in a box on the high desk. We sat on either side of the desk and I cupped my hands about the warm coffee cup. Salter looked haggard, as though he hadn't been to bed at all.

"The teletype reports you an unknown quantity, Withers," he began. "At least there's no record on you in Chicago."

"That's because their records don't go back beyond the fire."

He brooded over that, sipping on his coffee. The stubble of black beard emphasized his dusky qualities, drawing attention curiously enough to his really tiny forehead.

"What do you think really happened to Downey?" he asked finally.

"I think he eloped with Linda Brusick."

"Her father doesn't think so."

"You've seen Thumbs Brusick then. You know I wasn't making it all up?"

"Yeh, Brusick is in town. Temporarily. He hasn't heard anything from his daughter and he hasn't heard anything from Paddy Grogan."

"Paddy Grogan didn't have anything to do with it."

"I don't know. I just don't know. Brusick denied ever having heard of you, incidentally."

"Of course he did. That's so if those maniacs of his run me down he can be indifferent to the whole thing. But you know better."

"No I don't. I don't know a thing about you. All I know is that there have been two disappearances. At the moment, I still think you're trying to play up the coincidence to cover something about Downey. To tell the truth, I think you killed him." Salter pushed himself back from the desk and wandered to the window. "That's a sweet little town down there. Quiet even on a Saturday morning."

"What time is it, anyway?"

Salter brought his arm forward, pulled back the sleeve of his coat to expose the watch, but continued to gaze out the window for a still moment before he glanced down. "Just about noon," he said. "And I haven't been to bed all night."

"What the hell," I said with rising indignation. "I've missed Mass; don't you have a chaplain here?"

70

Salter shrugged without much sympathy, still caught in his somnolent reverie. "It's a sweet little town," he repeated. "And it's mine. It's all I have too. Stratford is my only wife, my only family." He gestured vaguely with his head. "I was born over there, on the other side of Front Street. It was a pretty tough neighborhood then, but it isn't now. I cleaned it up, almost singlehanded. Three nights running I led a group of the boys and we wiped out one dive after another. At the end of that week this town was mine."

Wearily he pulled out his cigarettes and a lighter; lighting a cigarette, he slumped against the window sill, still not looking at me. "You mark that down on the flap of your school book, Withers. This town is mine. I bled for it and that made it mine. Do you know what it means to be Chief of Detectives in Stratford? It means to be chief of yourself. I'm the sole member of the detective squad. Since I became chief there have been four mayors and two Chiefs of Police. They come and they go, but the town is mine.

"Stratford might not seem like a speck in the eye of Chicago, but it's big enough for me. Last night when you came staggering in here with your wild stories about Thumbs Brusick I almost turned sick. If those guys want to move in here there isn't a thing I could do about it. But Brusick wants nothing here but his daughter. And maybe one good shot at you. Well, I'm not going to cross those guys by trying to keep you from them. Technically I can keep you here until the courts open on Monday morning. I don't have to lay a charge on you at all, just keep you on suspicion in connection with the investigation of a murder."

"What murder? What murder? Who got murdered?" I spread my arms, palms up, in mock bewilderment. Salter turned from the window, hitching up his trousers, shrugging the sleep from his stolid body.

"I'm not going to keep you, though. I'm not going to force Thumbs Brusick and his guys into a show of strength. Have you got a place to hole up?"

"You're going to let me go now, is that it?"

"That is *not* it. I just don't want you gunned down in my jail. Do you have a hole in town that Brusick doesn't know about? What about the Barstairs, will they put you up?"

"They'll put me up."

"Okay. Come on, you can borrow the blanket."

Salter's car was black, powerful but undistinguished. It bore neither police identification nor special license plates. When we were pointed along Western Avenue he spoke with quiet menace.

"I want you to call the station every hour on the hour from now until I say so. And, Withers, they had better be local calls. If you try to get out of Stratford I'll turn Brusick on you with the simple request that he take you to the cut-and-fill dump three-and-one quarter miles out of my district. I swear that to you." He slowed the car down as he approached Bartie's house. "Is that the place?"

"The next house." I stepped out in front of Bartie's, and wrapped the blanket more securely about my shoulders.

He waited by the curb until he saw me push the door bell.

Bartie opened the door and squinted painfully at the bright sunlight. He wore a green eyeshade and came apparently from the microfilm viewer.

72

"Red?"

"Check."

"Gee, you look funny."

"Well, let me in before the neighbors start to laugh."

"All right, but be real quiet. Mary had a terrible shock last night, she was hysterial for hours. I know it didn't help the baby any. Something like that might mark the baby, you know what I mean? Not mark it, but imprint."

I pushed past him into the house, wadded the blanket and threw it on the unholy sofa.

"Listen, Bartie, is there any beer left?"

"I wouldn't even let her get up this morning, and I know that that isn't a good atmosphere for the baby, but. . . ." He trailed after me into the kitchen where I pulled open the refrigerator door and peered through the maze of milk bottles and refrigerated vitamin bottles. There was some beer.

"Bartie, dear? What is it, Bartie?" Mary, a robe pulled about her, appeared wanly at the door just as I turned from the icebox. For one long spluttering moment she stared at me, then she shrieked. "Maniac, maniac, maniac."

Bartie seized her hand and patted it. "Are you all right, dear? It's just Red. You remember Red, don't you? You remember him. You're all right now, dear. Are you all right?" Cautiously he steered her about, she moaning, and led her toward the bedroom.

"Bartie!" I called as the bedroom door closed. "*I* need you more than she does. It's all a sham. Bartie, *I* need you now. WHERE'S THE BEER CAN OPENER?" I rummaged through the drawers in the kitchen until I found a two-pronged fork that served with some pounding to open the beer can. The pounding suggested a useful occupation and I had just settled down on the kitchen floor to fix my loose heel with the potato masher when Bartie came back. He was pale and he began without preamble.

"You'll have to go."

"Can't Bartie."

"Please, Red, Mary says that you'll have to go and right away. The baby, you can't do this to my child. Be reasonable. I'm trying my best to prepare it for the birth trauma; it needs rest, and surely with Mary hysterical. . . ."

"Can't Bartie." I banged once more with the potato masher and he fairly danced with anxiety.

"Shush, quiet, stop that."

The heel seemed pretty secure by then; I slipped the shoe back on, stood and stamped my foot.

"Red, change your clothes and go. I simply will not tolerate this." The note of an aroused father sounding in Bartie's throat assured me that he was in earnest. I tried once more to appeal to his better nature.

"I spent the whole night in jail and now. . . ."

"You were running naked through the streets of Stratford last night; Mary saw you. Now look, I don't care what happened, just go for now. Can't you go back to Downey's house? I thought you were going to live there."

"Come on in while I change my clothes." I picked up the beer and headed for the front room, where I had left my suitcase the day before. It seemed clear that I would have to go. Where I would go or how I would call Salter every hour during the day I didn't know. "Can you lend me about forty-eight dimes?"

"What happened to the fifty dollars you got yesterday?"

"I thought you didn't want to know what happened."

"Well . . . will you leave if I lend you some money?"

I nodded. While I was dressing, putting on the wrinkled trousers and crumpled shirt from the suitcase, he fished out several dollar bills and weighed them judiciously in his hand. "It's only a loan," I said, and he handed them all to me. "Thanks." A thought struck me as I buttoned my shirt. "Bartie, tell me what you know about Jim Downey."

"Tell you what? He's a nice fellow, a scholar more than a teacher, I think. You know, shy."

"Where do you think he is now?"

"I don't know really; they say he ran off with Linda."

"Do you think that he did?"

"Well, if he did, she was the aggressor. She isn't his type at all."

"And what type is he?" I took off my shoes and pulled on a pair of socks.

"Shy, good, quiet. He's a daily communicant. That's why I find it hard to believe that he eloped. Oh, I know what passion is, but still the habit of grace and all that."

"Did you know that he's a dope addict?" I watched for the reaction on Bartie's face. He didn't even register faint indignation.

"No, he's not."

"And if I could offer proof?"

"Oh, Red, come off it; you couldn't offer proof . . . . I mean,

75

circumstantial evidence maybe, but not proof. He simply isn't. Furthest thing from truth."

"Are you sure?"

"Oh, yes." The accusation still struck him as so unsound as to bear little attention.

"Bartie, we know so little about our friends." He watched as I printed my name on a scrap of paper from his desk and stuffed it in my wallet with the money. I didn't want to be without identification again.

"Well, I confess you're a puzzle to me, but I never did profess knowing what makes you go. Downey is entirely different. He's quite a shallow fellow in many ways; I mean his depths are all pretty much spiritual ones, not complex twisted personality problems."

"Well yeah, I can see just how we're different. Tell me about Linda."

"She had a reputation for being rather, you know, wild?"

"How did Downey come to know her?"

"Well, it's a small college after all. I really didn't know that they knew each other, except that a teacher gets to know the names of most of the girls in the college."

"Bartie, it's important to me that Downey and Linda be found in the connubial hay — and soon. Where do you think they might be?"

"Now that we talk it over — air the problem, you know — I'm completely convinced that they haven't eloped. I never really did believe it, and I was going to call some authority, the police maybe, and score that hypothesis, but then Mary upset me. And I've been having trouble with the microfilm machine. I just haven't gotten around to it."

"At the moment then, the nuns at Saint Felicitas and I are the only ones who believe that Downey and Linda have eloped."

"I really know nothing about Linda," Bartie said. "Perhaps the police would know — or Linda's parents. You might make inquiries to one or the other of them."

I wrung Bartie's hand. He restored my faith in the monotony of life. Nothing wild or strange or hurtful could really happen. I wasn't threatened by mobsters and accused of murder by the police of Stratford. After all, Bartie and I inhabited the same world; it was for him a world in which nothing more exciting happened than a pregnancy, nothing more terrible than a burnt-out bulb in a microfilm viewer. His world was my world and so why was it that, as I walked to the front door, I felt sure that the ancient trees across the street concealed behind their scabby trunks (reading from left to right) Tabor, Thumbs Brusick, Chief of Detectives George Salter, and a certain leather-jacketed cab driver. At the door I turned back to Bartie.

"Just a lot of luck to you, brother."

"Why, thank you, Red. If there's anything I can do for you. . . ."

"Let me stay here."

"Anything but that, of course."

I slammed the door behind me in order to shut off what I felt sure were exulting cries from Mary, who was probably crouched painfully behind the bedroom door all the time I was dressing. I might have been unjust; she might truly have been trying to go to sleep, in which case the slamming of the door would have had the effect of waking her. Good thing in the long run; if she slept less during the day she would probably sleep better at night.

Cautiously I walked to the corner. I peered behind none of the trees, but I expended effort in stifling the temptation. At the corner I realized that I was free from watchers. Now, where to go? I knew less than half a dozen places in Stratford, the cottage, the bar, the jail — every one of those places was probably watched by Brusick mobsters. I suddenly resolved that I would no longer be a pawn, lurking about in danger until the game was played. The simplest thing was to discover Linda and Downey for myself. Surely, *someone* must know their plans. Downey might be a tight-lipped, hypocritical hophead — public opinion to the contrary — but Linda was a woman — her position as a student at Saint Felicitas supported that contention — and she *must* have confided in someone. The nuns were, with me, convinced that an elopement had taken place; what did they know?

Toward the college I now directed my firm and steady steps. I saw no one on my way. From a distance came the smell of burning leaves and the sharp, bird-like cries of children at play; but the avenue leading to the college was deserted. The campus, too, seemed devoid of life.

I made straight for the Administration Building, only to find the front door locked. I prowled first to my right, along the walls of the classroom wing. All was locked and barred. To the left, things looked more promising. A few giant strides to the rear of the left wing of the Administration Building was the two-storied red brick dormitory. Here a door was unlocked. I pushed cautiously in.

It was a large gloomy room I entered, its walls pretty well covered with dark oleo prints of virgin martyrs. Straight ahead a narrow wooden stairway led upward; I started for that.

"May I hep yew?" A tight voice called.

I swung guiltily around. There, behind the telephone switchboard, but very much on her dignity, sat a prim young shrew, my way to bar.

"Yes, of course. I would like to speak with one of the Sisters, Sister Mary Ransom perhaps."

"The Sisters are all on retreat this week end. If you will cumb bach Sunday evening?"

"Oh? Well, that's a disappointment. I wonder if perhaps Linda Brusick had a roommate?"

"Yew mean Carol O'Connor, of course."

"Of course."

"Of course." That seemed to end the conversation; the little shrew returned to the book that she had propped open on the switchboard.

"I'll just have a few words with Carol."

I had apparently committed the breach for which she was prepared. She smiled with prim malice and her accent changed. "You may not see her. You are not allowed into the dormitory of course, and I am not allowed to call a girl unless it is for a member of the family who has sent notice of his impending arrival. Saturday mornings are study periods here."

"Ah? Well, perhaps I could make a telephone call?"

"Not on the house phone."

"Naturally, my dear Cerbera. An outside call."

I dialed information and asked the number of the police telephone. "116," the information operator replied, and without further ado connected me with the police department.

"Police," rasped a husky voice.

"May I speak to Chief of Detectives Salter?" There was a moment's pause. I rolled my eyes at the prissy switchboard operator.

"Is this Withers?"

"Yes. Yes, it is."

"Okay, that will do. No need to call the chief." There was a space of silence, then the dial signal came across the wire firm and clear. I had been cut off. I continued to hold the phone to my ear, pressing it tighter so that the prim little girl could not hear the buzz.

"That's right," I said into the phone, "I'm here now . . . You know how I stand on that. I'd hate to put them all under house arrest. . . . Yes, of course, but the operator here, she . . . Well, of course, she's obstructing justice, but we can't . . . No, no, don't send the boys just yet; let me give them one more chance . . . Okay, Q.E.D. signing off." I hastily dropped the phone back on its hook.

"Em sure the Sisters would wish me to cooperate with officers of the lawr," the little girl said.

80

"Well, I'm pretty sure of that myself. Just give me the number of Carol O'Connor's room."

"The rooms don't halve numbers; she and Linda Brusick share 'Saint Hilda', but men are not allowed upstairs."

I started for the stairs, then turned deliberately back. "Have it your way then. Just let me use the phone once more, if you will. Then you can go and pack a little bag for the week end if you wish. I'll watch the switchboard here. You'll need toothbrush, nightie. . . ."

The Eastern accent, so carefully cultivated in the wastes of Indiana, was once more beginning to slip. "Wull, if you're really an investigator."

"I am."

"Is it about Linda?"

"It is."

"I guess you can. . . ."

"That's right."

I stalked up the stairs; ahead of me lay a narrow corridor lined with doors, the first labeled "Saint Ethelreda," the next on my left, "Saint Bridget." I followed the hagiographic alphabet to "Saint Hilda." There the door was partially ajar; the other doors had been closed. From most of them came the sounds of radio music.

I knocked quietly; there was no response. Slowly I pushed the door open until I could see the whole room. There were two beds, one neatly made, one rumpled; both bore several large stuffed animals. A pile of clothes lay beside the rumpled bed. Two desks by the window seemed equally cluttered; across the only comfortable chair a camel's hair coat was thrown. The room was unoccupied.

I stepped in, pulled the door partially closed behind me and strode to the medicine chest over the minute wash basin in the corner. I opened the mirrored door and was confronted with an unbelievable array of cosmetic jars, jugs, tubes, bottles, and silvered envelopes. There was no chamois cloth bag such as I had found in Downey's medicine chest. On the bottom shelf, however, there were three leather razor boxes of the kind that enclose delicate feminine razors. Three razors and two roommates added up to some sort of indecency. I reached for the first case just as I heard the door swing open behind me. I whirled to confront Carol O'Connor.

She was tall and tawny and her hair, a natural curly chestnut, clung about her face. She wore a gabardine trench coat buttoned to the chin and scuffed loafers. Her legs were bare. She stopped in the doorway, a startled doe — or perhaps a wary tiger. I am not strong in the area of interpreting feminine moods. I did feel, however, that Carol was trying to convey an image, either of a cat or a deer, or perhaps a koala bear. I mean, I felt that there was something rehearsed in her startled response. Maybe all young women practice being startled; I know that it is not well done unless one has practiced. I had made a sad show before Thumbs Brusick. Anyway, she posed in the doorway, indicating surprise.

"It's all right," I said. "I'm conducting a survey."

"What are you doing here?" she asked.

"I just answered that, didn't I? I've been hired by Sister Ransom (a mental reservation there) and I'm making a survey."

"What are you doing at my medicine chest?"

"Yes, that, well I'm making a survey. It's for my family's business. We want to know what kind of cough drops college women use."

There was a glint of laughter in the dark eyes. "Are you really a descendant of the Smith Brothers?"

"Oh, no. My uncle was named Lydia Pinkham. He *used* to have a beard, but then he got to drinking his own stuff." Carol swung the door open wider.

"I don't know what you want, but you had better get out of here."

"But look, what about my survey?"

"If you don't get out of here immediately I'm going to call Sister."

"Good, what are you going to call her?"

She laughed. I think she wasn't frightened for the simple reason that she outweighed me by several pounds. On the other hand (that flattering hand so readily extended in my behalf), the truth seemed to be that I didn't really project such an image of evil as Salter seemed to believe. Of course, I wasn't trying; I was trying to ingratiate myself.

"Really, I'm here because of Linda." The laughter died in her throat.

"Linda?" She stepped into the room and swung the door closed. "What do you know about Linda? Is she all right?"

"Rats, that's what I was going to ask." I snapped open

83

the razor case in my hand and saw a delicate gold razor. I turned back to reach for another of the three cases as Carol crossed the room to drop wearily on the nearer bed.

"It's the one on the left," she said. After a moment she asked. "Isn't that what you're looking for?"

I glanced down at the razor box in my hand. Slowly I opened it to find a hypodermic needle and a small, blackened silver child's spoon. Dumbly I nodded.

"Are you from the police?"

"I am," I answered huskily. I was, after all, *from* the police.

"I don't believe it," Carol said. She was blind to nuances and mental reservations.

"Well, as a matter of fact, I'm an English instructor at good old Saint Felicitas." Carol sighed in response and then turned her hands palm upward on her lap. She studied her palms as she spoke.

"I've spent ages, really ages and ages, worrying about the moment when a strange man would walk into this room and find Linda's kit. You know, I've imagined myself in every conceivable position: studying, combing my hair, even in bed. I thought, perhaps, the most embarrassing and difficult thing would be for him to walk in when I had a mouthful of toothpaste. And I pictured the man too; I imagined every type: rough, friendly, fatherly, mean. But never for one moment did I think that it would be a clown."

I thought it best to ignore her thoughtless remarks. "Your performance at the door did look a little rehearsed."

She nodded wearily. "It was; at least mentally, it was. I

need a fag." She arose from the bed and rummaged through the clutter on the desk for a packet of cigarettes. I think her use of the word *fag* did more to break down my natural reserve than anything else. I mean, on the campuses that I inhabited cigarettes haven't been called *fags* since nineteen-ought-eight. Would she ask me for a Lucifer match next? I realized suddenly the backwater of the genteel finishing school. Little did Sister Ransom realize what turbulence she had introduced into her brackish pond. She who had hired Red Withers would be held accountable when the students began winning regularly on football pools, when the students found themselves enmeshed in contemporary argot. And then I thought, how unreal must have seemed the wisdom of this little world to poor Linda Brusick, fresh from her father's board.

Carol had taken a wrinkled pack of cigarettes from the cluttered desk; now she shook one loose and lit it. To light the cigarette she canted her head to the right in an engaging fashion that set off the chestnut curls against the smoothness of her face. It struck me that most of her movements had been rehearsed. How often had she practiced that gesture? Or was it a natural gesture to one of her unassuming beauty? She inhaled expertly — *that* took practice I knew — and sat again on the edge of the bed.

"Anyway, I'm glad it's over, whoever you are. It's been terrible."

"This is Linda's kit?" Carol nodded. "Where's yours?"

"I don't have any. I never once in my whole life. . . ."

"Okay, then why tell me how terrible it's been?"

"You don't know what it is to live with a person who's using narcotics. You don't know how Linda has changed in three months. I don't think she even looks like she did three months ago. She doesn't use make-up anymore, except for eye paint. And she wears those black, long-sleeved sweaters — to hide her arms, you know. But it's more than that. Linda has really changed." Carol shook her head wearily.

"Is she really an addict?"

"She is. She doesn't think so, but she is." Carol ground out the cigarette and immediately lit another. I didn't feel that I could sit on the same bed that she perched on, nor on the chair that bore in addition to the camel's hair coat several unidentifiable wisps of nylon, lace and elastic. I contented myself with lounging back against the porcelain sink.

"Why didn't you report her? Tell somebody?"

"Ha, you don't know Linda. She thought she could stop any time she wanted to, and she had me convinced right up until this month. Then, it was just too terrible. You can't just walk up to a nun and say. . . . Well, what would you say? Never mind, I was wrong. Did you come down here with her father?" I shook my head. "Well, I didn't think that I could tell *him*. Oh, I was wrong, I know it, that's what I've been saying to myself for three days now. Over and over again I've been saying it."

"Okay, I'm not blaming you. But listen, was it because of dope that she and Downey ran off together."

"They didn't run off together. I don't know what happened, but they didn't run off together."

"It's important to me that they did. How can you be so sure?"

"Do you know what the kids call him? Amelia Cecilia. Professor Amelia Cecilia Downey. I don't think that Linda even knew him. Oh, she was signed up for one of his classes I guess, but she hasn't gone to very many classes at all. And she *was* such a wonder before. Linda had magnetism. You wouldn't understand but I love that girl. We're both art majors, and in every class Linda was the core, the center. She had vitality and life and joy and happiness. We spent almost every day together, all day long, classes in the morning, the studio in the afternoon. . . . Oh, that's why she took one of Doctor Downey's classes. The art majors take some of their classes in the evening because of the studio work every afternoon. But it's ridiculous to think that she loved Doctor Downey."

"He's an addict too."

She snorted at that; it was a sweet and charming snort. But a snort.

"He was not. Look, I've lived with an addict. *I* know what it's like. The only narcotics Doctor Downey ever experienced were his own lectures."

"How come nobody else knew about Linda if she was so changed? Isn't there a Sister Hall Prowler in the dormitory?"

Linda glanced uneasily at the closed door. "Maybe I'd better open the door, huh?"

"In a minute; tell me first."

"Well, she always had black moods. You know who her father is? Sometimes that got her down and she'd kind of go into a shell. I guess they just haven't noticed how long she's been down."

"Where is she?"

"I don't know, really I don't. That's why I feel so guilty." She fumbled about on the bed for the cigarettes but came up instead with a wadded handkerchief with which she took a mean swipe at her nose.

"Are you sure that Linda and Downey didn't clutch each other and trot off as one?"

"I *know*. Linda disappeared Wednesday morning. Doctor Downey was still around on Thursday. I saw him on campus."

"I thought they both dropped from sight on Thursday."

"I made bed check for Linda Wednesday night. I've done that a lot lately. I told Sister that Linda was in the shower but present and accounted for. Usually Linda sneaked up the fire escape about midnight."

I remembered the telephone call that I had so sleepily answered at Bartie's house; someone, some girl, had been looking for Downey late Thursday night.

"Are you sure Downey was on campus?"

"Sure."

"And anyone could have seen him?"

"Sure."

"But Linda wasn't on campus?"

"No."

And according to Sister Ransom's check, Linda was the only girl missing. Then it was probably Linda who had called, and that call confirmed my belief, in the face of Carol's objections, that their disappearance was joint.

"Who was Linda out with those nights she didn't make bed check?"

88

"Nobody in particular. She used to hang out at the *Pardonnez Moi.* That's a beatnik joint in Stratford; you know, very arty, very hip."

"Is that where she got the dope?"

"I don't know. I don't think so. I've thought and thought about it. But usually I come back to the same old questions: What should I have done? Why didn't I tell somebody?" Carol ran her hand nervously across the rumpled bed. It was clear that neither cigarette nor hanky quite answered her need. I stood upright; the difference in height was imperceptible but I was poised for flight.

"Are you going to tell about Linda now?" I asked. She shrugged her shoulders, still plucking idly at the bed. I don't think she looked up as I slipped out of the room.

Chapter 5

WITH INFINITE CARE I padded about the edge of the marshy lake. My makeshift elevator shoes, their laces tied together, I bore about my neck; my socks were stuffed in my pocket. My bare feet made no sound as they fell upon the harsh grasses, upon pebbles and broken beer bottles, aspirin tins and similar metal containers that edged the lake. The only sounds were the soft cries of pain that escaped my pressed lips. I hoped to approach Downey's cottage from the unused front yard, to spy upon any possible spies. I thought it imperative that I learn just how sincere Thumbs Brusick was in his intention to drop me. A guard at Downey's cottage would surely reveal the firmness of his purpose. If the house was deserted and unobserved, I hoped to wait there until dusk announced the opening of the doors of *Pardonnez Moi.*

The quest was something more than a matter of curiosity now, and it was something more than an effort to clear myself with the law and the underworld at once. Jim Downey and Linda Brusick had so etched themselves on my memory that

I knew I had to uncover the real persons. If there were clues I would follow them; if there were no clues I would busily seek suggestions. No scholar in passionate pursuit of introduced-error-in-the-text felt more deeply toward his quest than I toward mine. Downey was my alter ego, the figure after whom I could cry, "There but for the grace of God and the cunning of my curricular misplotting, go I." Linda's magnetism drew me as it had drawn her roommate. I had to know what had happened. Simply to flee—say, to the safety of the wilderness—struck me as impossibly ludicrous. Somehow, for the first time in my life, I was *engaged*, caught in the human maelstrom.

Foolish I might have been in the ways of the world, but to my own astonishment I proved wise in the cunning of the bush. My choice of a devious route to the lakeside cottage proved a sterling one, for I saw, while yet concealed by the wet pine brush, a figure. It was a toad-like figure, a squat ugly man dressed in black crouching in the grasses at the corner of the cottage. "Tabor," I inwardly cried, even as my face stung with memory of his foul punch.

That silent black figure meant a number of things to me. For one, it meant that the intended Brusick-Grogan meeting had not been accomplished; for another, it meant that Brusick held firm purpose of doing me wilful, irreparable harm. It meant that Linda Brusick was still missing and unaccounted for. It meant that I had nowhere to await the dusk. I turned silently in the brush, a foreshortened Natty Bumppo, and made back to the campus.

"The Movies," I thought, as I passed through the main

gates of the campus and started down Western Avenue. A movie house would be an ideal spot to spend the afternoon. I thought it prudent to stay off the main streets and so turned to my left away from Western. But then it occurred to me that Brusick was no fool. If he had his thugs looking for me, they would be prowling the side streets on the assumption that I wouldn't dare walk the main drags. I cut back to Western Avenue after several blocks.

But the strain was too great. After two blocks on Western Avenue I turned to walk again on a parallel side street of little importance. The sound of every approaching automobile brought my heart into my throat and made my beard bristle with electricity. Six or seven blocks from the campus I was a wreck; and then it occurred to me that there were probably no neighborhood movies in a town the size of Stratford. I had, undoubtedly, seen all the theaters in town when I had seen the two opposing marquees in Main Street. No bearded man, and he a hunted man, could walk through the little town that far unnoted.

Then I saw the A & P supermarket. There, I felt, I would be safe from Brusick; he would never think to look for me in the crowd of Saturday shoppers. I pushed into the market, changed one of Bartie's dollar bills at the check-out stand and called the police station again.

"Hallo," I said, "I'm calling Chief. . . ."

"Is that Withers?" It was the same raspy voice that I had heard an hour before.

"Yes. Withers here."

"You're fifteen minutes late."

"Right. You know, a man with your powers of observation shouldn't be on the switchboard. Is it jealousy in high places that keeps you there?"

"Okay, wise guy, do you know what Chief of Detectives Salter told me to do if you call in late again?"

"No, but if *I* were you, I'd notify the police." I hung up. Now my problem was to while away the time in the supermarket until it became good dusk outside. Then I could venture the streets again and seek out *Pardonnez Moi*.

I chose a wire market cart and began trundling it down the first long corridor. The shelves were more than head-high, crammed with cans in brightly colored labels, packed with glass jars that showed ingeniously packed olives, pickles, fruits and nuts. There seemed miles and miles of such corridors; thousands of cans and boxes cried out to me to be seized and carried off. I gave in easily, a purposeless mariner glad of the diversion afforded by the siren's flamboyant cries. Lulled by the seductive music that crept from corners, enticed by pictures, by special prices and free gifts, I rapidly filled a wire cart, which I was forced to abandon near the meat counter. Quickly I returned to the front of the store and pulled for a second cart. That I wheeled smartly to the other end of the store and again gave in to the advertising. I filled that cart as rapidly as the first, and this one I abandoned just beyond the fresh vegetables.

A third and fourth cart I filled until, satiated, I halted. It was bad for me, I realized, to give in to each impulse; I was destroying the tough fiber of the inner man. And I was in danger of clogging the aisles with my abandoned wire carts.

Once again I started at the front of the store; this time I chose judiciously. If I found two or three brands of the same item, I read the labels carefully before choosing the least expensive brand. At the olive counter I spent a great deal of time counting the number of olives in each of the variously shaped jars. The prices seemed to bear little relationship to the quantities. Perhaps in green olives there was a subtle but important taste differential that I had never been able to detect and it was this that accounted for the differences in price.

Before the array of dehydrated dog foods I almost broke down, trying to evaluate the relative merits of each brand against the weight and price of the box. There were simply too many differentials to account for: protein percentages, water content, percentage of fat, added vitamins, analyses of mineral content. It was too much, and I decided against taking any dog food at all.

My feet grew weary and my legs more weary yet. Ever and again I wheeled my cart past a demonstration booth and was offered a minute piece of sausage on a wooden toothpick. That sustained my strength for a while. The market seemed to tolerate every conceivable eccentricity of dress and quirk of behavior save one. No one in the store was allowed to sit. Like so many powerless barges, the customers were towed musically up one aisle and down the other, then driven through the terrible locks of the check-out stands.

For a while I thought that eating, too, was forbidden; anyone eating in a supermarket looks guilty. But I found that I could safely eat by standing close to the demonstration display amid the musing customers who were munching on their tiny sausage bits. I drove purposefully to the delicatessen counter, whirled back and parked my cart close to the sausage display. Then, looking aloft, brooding apparently on prices and menus, I contentedly ate a dill pickle, a package of luncheon meats, a small packet of crackers and a quarter pound of Longhorn cheese. The cellophane in which my supper had been wrapped I tidily wrapped into a ball and deposited on the far side of the store behind the cabbage display.

It was there that I found an added diversion—and quite by chance. I was standing by the fresh vegetables when I first felt a timid presence behind me. Cautiously I turned; it was a very youthful *Hausfrau* in checkered shirt and blue jeans. She held in her hands two exotic-looking autumnal squashes.

"Could you tell me what these are?"

"Ah, yes," I said pointing at random to the one in her left hand, "That is an acorn squash and the other is, an, um, thyroid pumpkin." I had to rely on free association for the latter.

"Do you know how I should go about cooking them?"

"Well, prepare them just the way you would a pumpkin: wash them, rub them with butter or oil and put them in the oven, a medium over, for about forty minutes. Or until they have risen to about twice their size." The advice seemed, perhaps, a bit too familiar to her; she hesitated, decided against both, thanked me and moved away.

But my diversion had been introduced. For the next half an hour or so I stood by the vegetables, close to the squashes peculiar to the autumn, and stared judiciously down at the heaped up piles. Again and again I was approached by shoppers, and not always were they pretty young brides. My opinion was solicited on the selection and preparation of nearly every kind of fruit and vegetable exhibited in the section. I gave advice and recipes readily until simultaneously invention left me and the department manager began hovering near. I shoved off for the secluded paper-goods sections and a quiet think.

Carol O'Connor's evidence struck me as valid, and I finally abandoned the contention that Linda Brusick's disappearance and the disappearance of Jim Downey were linked. They had dropped independently from sight; only coincidence and the romantic imagination of Sister Ransom had connected the two disappearances. This opinion united me with Thumbs Brusick and with Chief of Detectives George Salter. But not too closely; Salter's accusation of murder was obviously foolish. Was Thumbs Brusick's theory of a Grogan kidnapping as far-starry as George Salter's theory of murder? Or, and more to the point, would I be forced to lurk in the Stratford A & P until not one, but both, of the wanderers were returned?

I was jostled by a man reaching for a roll of shelf paper. Wise in the ways of the supermarket, I jostled back, determined to give as good as I got.

"Oh, Mr. Withers? I'm sorry." The voice was bland and unctious, as colorless as the face that matched it and from which the sounds escaped. It was the pale student from the evening class, the quiet gentleman whom I remembered from classes at Chicago U.

"Well, it's a tiny world, isn't it?" I said. As a matter of fact,

I was at a loss for words. His calling me by name while I was so complacently pretending to be incognito had put a burr under my tongue.

"Anyway, Stratford is a pretty small place. I didn't get a chance to tell you how much I enjoyed your lecture last night; but I knew that we would meet frequently if you were to stay at Saint Felicitas."

"Well, thank you." I am vain of my humble responses.

"You certainly threw new light on Riley. And Dante. It wasn't clear to me — my fault entirely — I'm sure you made the point sufficiently plain, but I'm not as attentive as I should be—whether you said that Dante or Riley had written 'The Congo.'"

"Ah yes, 'Mumbo Jumbo.'"

"That's the poem. Of course, I'm not familiar with Italian and I suppose that I miss much of the true flavor of such phrases."

"I suppose. . . . Listen, are you pulling my leg?"

"Pardon?" He met my glance directly and it occurred to me that the gaze was not so much bland as veiled. Surely at Chicago or Stratford or at one of the many college extension classes that he had attended he would have learned something.

"Well, never mind. I didn't get your name last night."

"I thought perhaps that you had it on the class roll. I'm Edward West." He replaced the paper roll and extended his hand. We shook hands cordially.

"Glad to see you here. Give a cheer for old Chicago and all that, what? Did you move to Stratford?"

"I was transferred, actually," he said.

My cordiality was forced. I had held semiprofessional students in contempt too long to change even when I was in need of a dispassionate friend. And I have always carried an active animosity for people who use the word *actually*. I resolved to remove myself, but then the thought struck me that he might know more about Stratford than I could find out in an evening at *Pardonnez Moi*.

"What's your line, West?" I smiled ingratiatingly, but I received only a humorless glance.

"I'm a representative for sewing machine parts. Call on manufacturers' representatives, that sort of thing. Actually, I'm not very good at it, but the parts sell themselves. The company moves me about a good deal. Well, actually, not *that much*. I mean, Stratford, Chicago, Dubuque, but not in that order."

"Do you know a place called the *Pardonnez Moi*?"

"Oh?" He stopped and plucked a cellophaned pack of paper napkins from the bottom shelf before he answered.

"Did I say a dirty word?" I asked.

"No, no. I just wondered where you had learned of that place. It's pretty much, well, a dive."

"One of the girls at school mentioned it."

"As a matter of fact, I go there quite a lot myself. I mean, actually Stratford doesn't have much to offer after Chicago." He hadn't brought his wire cart into the paper lane, so he stood there holding the napkins conspicuously before him.

"What kind of a place is it?" I asked.

"Not quiet exactly. Actually most of the clientele are artists. That type, anyway. There are poetry and jazz readings now and then. Bongo drums. Folk songs. What was the name of the girl who recommended it?"

I strove for the flat and nasal tone that would show him that we were two of a kind. "Actually, she didn't *recommend* the place."

"Ah?"

"Yes, she just said that it was there. But she didn't say where."

"Oh. Well, you know the movie houses? It's back of the *Isis,* about three blocks or so toward the river."

"Would the place be open now?"

"I suppose so. Why?"

"I thought I might go there. Did you by any chance meet a Linda Brusick there? I mean anytime?"

"I don't know any of the names." He paused, glanced down at his package. "I'll toddle off with my paper napkins, I guess. Was she the girl who recommended the place?"

"No." It was on the tip of my tongue to say that she was the girl who had run off with Downey. "No," I said, "not she."

"I actually wouldn't know her."

"I suppose not. On the other hand, maybe you would. She was in the class you are taking at old Saint Felicitas."

"I don't think that I know her. Is she a heavy girl?"

"That I couldn't say. Well, listen, it's been fine to meet you; see you next week." I was already bent for the nitery, if that is what the *Pardonnez Moi* was.

Edward West and I waved sheepish hands as I turned away. I realized, as I strode toward the check-out stand, that

I couldn't simply nod to the cashier. To leave a supermarket empty-handed was even more heinous than sitting down in one. I seized the nearest nearly empty basket and shoved it under the cash register trough. There were three untended wire carts near the stand; one was nearly full, one was the one I had been filling, and the one I chose was nearly empty. The one I grabbed promised the least drain on my pocketbook. The cashier smiled professionally and began flicking packages onto the counter. Arrogantly she rang up the price, singing out the cost of each in an unintelligible voice. I paid for a pound of coffee, a pound of orange pekoe tea and three pounds of sugar.

"That is powdered sugar. Do you want the granulated?" the cashier asked, her hand poised over the keys of the register.

"No, no. Just what's there, thank you." I counted out the change as a pimply-faced boy sacked my purchases. I knew that some purchaser would be forced to begin again with her selection, after a moment or two of distress that might in the long run be good for her. I carried my sack to the telephone booth and never looked at it again. In the booth, I dropped a dime into the slot of the telephone, dialed 116 and heard the familiar voice respond, "Stratford Police Department."

"This is Chief of Detectives George Salter. May I speak to Red Withers, and reverse the charges." I hung up before his undoubtedly profane reply could offend me.

The gathering dusk gave me confidence and I strolled rather than trotted in the direction of the heart of Stratford. At the first busy intersection I turned to the left and toward the river. Three blocks and then a fourth for good measure I walked before I turned again in the direction of the business district. If Edward West's directions were accurate, I should come to *Pardonnez Moi* in another five or six blocks. This was a residential district; the infrequent street lamps, recently lit, flickered through heavy trees. The walks were deserted and my journey was marked by the baying of half-earnest watchdogs. Had I a dog of my own, or a pipe to taint the crisp autumnal air, such a pleasant stroll past quiet houses would have brought me relaxed thoughts of the brooding verities: life, death, taxes, literature and love. As it was, I thought on justice.

I had chided Carol O'Connor for not reporting that her roommate was a narcotics addict. But then, wasn't I guilty of the same offense in not reporting what I knew of Jim Downey? Was her offense terrible, mine negligible, because she knew the offender and I didn't? But reflecting thus was no way to give me the courage and confidence to pursue my quest. I would have to be stern with myself and forbid such thoughts. I would simply have to adopt the bourgeois attitude that had for so long sustained my ancestors. There are two standards of conduct, one for people at large, and one for myself. Circumstances and interior pressures might on occasion compel me to cheat a little, and lie a smidgen, and be the teeniest bit of a schnook, but the good Lord knew that I always intended the best for myself.

I felt somehow closer to my own past, to my ancestors who had conned the Roman legionnaires, who had run from the Anglo-Saxons, who had hidden from the French at the battle of Agincourt. I felt warmly akin to the large-hearted Withers who had first turned a brave face to the New World and had come to America to avoid debt, and who had set out for the frontiers in the new world at the first sounds of musket fire in the Revolutionary War. Stratford, Indiana, of a brisk evening in autumn seemed to represent the very heart of America, and somehow it seemed appropriate that here a Withers should be skulking down back streets.

It was suddenly good to be alive and I resolved to preserve the feeling. Heaven knows I had proved my courage in the war. Bravery itself had coupled in my breast with fear of the law and I had reported unflinchingly to the draft board. It *must* have been bravery. "It was guts," I said aloud and a new dog barked.

I had done my part in the war. Night after night I had shouldered my rifle and had solemnly mounted guard. It was at a military camp in Kansas, within a stone's throw of the geographical center of the United States, but my heart was high and my pulse steady as I tramped around and around the sleeping barracks, protecting my fellows-in-arms from heaven alone knew what. In quiet exhilaration, brought on by the memory of my past bravery, I picked up a stone and shied it at a street lamp. My aim was true and brave. In the shattering sound of the breaking street lamp and the sudden darkness punctuated by the wild barking of a nearby dog, I broke into a brisk trot, turned the corner sharply to my right as I saw porch lights flick on, and there before me was the *Pardonnez Moi.*

It had been a warehouse, a small and apparently unused

warehouse, before it had been remodeled. The ancient brick front was covered with carefully selected, witty graffiti. A single light globe illumined the swinging wooden board that proclaimed its name. The illumination within was similar; here and there throughout the high-ceilinged room hung single, naked light globes. The tables were small and crowded close together, the chairs—four or five to a table— were of multiple design and of disreputable pasts. To the rear I could see a large and evil-looking espresso machine, its copper cover dented and blackened, the pipes leading upwards at crazy angles, its front pimpled with valves and knobs. I chose a table near the wall and halfway to the rear.

Perhaps half the tables were occupied, one or two young people sprawled and entwined about the chairs that were clustered around each table. At first glance the occupants seemed all to be dressed alike in grey duffle coats, but as my eyes grew accustomed to the smoke and gloom I realized that some few impostors were wearing grey jackets or top coats. They all seemed to converse only by gesture, for the silence was heavy, until one of the young men bent forward over what appeared to be but didn't sound like a guitar and began in a dreadful and piercing whine to cry out the song, "John Henry." A few heads turned in his direction but most of the gloomy occupants continued to commune with each other with intense gazes.

I was hardly surprised by the scene. After all, I had been watching undergraduate aberrations for years and years. I was surprised, however, that Stratford could turn out so many of the popular type. The patois, I would soon discover, was ersatz, but it was a credit to the local press that knowledge of the right thing had been so widely disseminated through the rank and file of Stratfordians, for surely not all of these could be college students. The waitress surprised me however; she was dressed in black leotards and a pony tail.

"Good grief, child, a negative of you would be banned in Boston."

"Boston," she sneered. It was a verbal trick that I heard frequently that night. The trick was simply to repeat, with infinite disdain, the last word addressed to you.

"Well, let's see what I'd like to drink."

"Drink," she sneered.

"Ah? Well, in that case only a beer."

"Beer!" with a turn of the pretty pouting lips.

"Don't tell me that I have stumbled into a nest of teetotalers?"

"Teetotalers?!"

I resolved to break the chain, bad luck or not.

"The atmosphere here is positively antedeluvian."

"You can have a beer," she said, but she was beaten.

The folk songs continued with disquieting regularity; the tables began to fill. Saturday night was apparently the big night at the *Pardonnez Moi*. The latecomers were forced to sit at tables already occupied. They were a congenial group and no one seemed to mind. I did, of course. The first couple who approached my table I drove away with a salacious leer. The second couple was more determined, but I promptly pinched the girl as she sat and they removed themselves to a table in the far corner. In time the empty chairs at my table were carried away and I was left the sole possessor of the only private table in the joint. Late in the evening, conversation broke suddenly forth. If it were by pre-arranged signal I did not catch the signal, but at once all seemed to be talking. The babble was not quite so unpleasant as the nasal folk songs.

Once when the dark sylph of a waitress paused to serve another beer she told me, "Like listen, man, we've had two complaints against you already. So watch it."

"Id!" I said. She took a moment to digest it.

"Say, like you're all right."

"No, child, you should have said with withering scorn, 'Id!' Incidentally, my name is Withers, Scorn Withers, and I'm looking for Linda Brusick. Do you know her?"

"Name me no names. What does she look like?"

"She's one of the college mob, an art major; comes here a lot. She's the one who cut the scene after curfew many a time."

She picked up the nearly empty beer bottle and drained the contents into my glass. "Like, I might know and I might not. What else about her?"

"She has a monkey on her back."

"I know."

"Is she here tonight?"

"No, but see the fat cat with the guitar?" She gestured with a black-sheathed hip. "The trouper over there? He and Linda swing."

"Would you ask him to cut over here?"

She studied me a moment through lowered lashes. "You're not the Fuzz?"

"No. Just ask him to come over and bring his own chair." I watched her work through the close-packed chairs. The guitarist glanced in my direction, then he lifted his chair over his head and wiggled his way through the crowd to my table. He placed his chair across for me and sat examining his guitar. I waited until it seemed clear that I would have to be the first to speak.

"Do you want a beer?"

He shook his head and plucked at the guitar. Beneath the regulation duffel coat he wore a dark turtle-neck sweater; his hair was long, black and full. There was about his sallow cheeks what looked like a day's growth of dark beard, but might have been a week's growth if he were as young as I suspected. I tried once again to get a response from him.

"How did a silent type like you ever get the reputation of being a wit?"

He looked up, but the light was too poor for me to read much in his eyes.

"Who say?"

"Who do you think? Don't you swing with Linda?"

"You know Linda?"

Sooner or later one of us would have to answer in a declarative statement.

"You her contact?" I jutted my beard at him and leaned forward across the table. He pulled backward and in that gesture I read his age: rising twenty.

"Man, I don't touch the stuff."

"Doesn't prove."

"Look, man, that junk, it's terrible stuff. I'm Straightsville."

"I got a car outside. Let's just run down to the station." I stood and drained my beer glass.

"Man, that's wild talk. I don't even smoke pot. Look, somebody gave you a wrong tip. Honestly. . . ."

"Okay, so I'm wrong. Your folks can bail you out Monday morning." The beatific pose was gone, an earnest young boy gazed up at me in near despair.

"Gee, listen, this can't be. My old lady will flip."

I stared at him as though weighing his merits. "Can I be sure that you'll level with me?"

"Anything, but don't haul me in. Honestly, I never so much as once touched junk."

I settled back in my chair. It occurred to me that I had dominated him in part by glaring down at him; that was a feat I could pull off only with a seated adversary. My success this time was complete and I wondered if God hadn't been wise in making me only five-foot-almost-three. What a demagogue I would have been at five and a half; the scourge of the world at six feet. Seven feet would have made me the first American pope.

"How well do you know Linda?"

"Yeh, well, I'm mixed up with her, but only on the set. I mean, we always meet here and she takes a taxi back to Booksville."

"When was the last time you saw her?"

"Oh, man, it's been days." A couple forcing their way

through the press of tables patted him on the back as they passed. Half turning his head, he muttered a flat, inflectionless "Crazy, crazy." They laughed loudly and pushed on.

"What do you mean, days?"

"It was Tuesday, I think. Yeh, Tuesday she was here. She was way out then. Madsville, you know? I haven't been back since."

"Did you make any plans to see her again?"

"No, man, nothing like that. You know, we just swung out whenever we could."

"How badly was she hooked?"

"All the way. Like she was mainlining it."

"Why didn't you tell us about it?"

"Huh?" the question seemed really to puzzle him.

"Why didn't you rat on her? Why didn't you tell? Never mind, I know why. You thought she was smart; you thought she was really swinging, didn't you?"

"She was, man, she was."

"Someday you'll know better. Anyway, I hope so. Who was her contact?"

"I don't know."

"Does she get the stuff here?"

"I don't know. I suppose so. Look man, like I say, I'm pure-o."

"Oh, no."

"Are you going to arrest me?"

I shook my head at the way of the world. "I'm the fugitive, old Truepenny."

I pushed back from the table, pushed through the crowd

108

and walked to the door. All my sympathy for the poor goaded pair, Jim Downey and Linda Brusick, had come to a head and had burst. I was emotionally drained, physically exhausted. The door of *Pardonnez Moi* swung to behind me and I turned wearily toward town. My feet dragged, the double heels swishing through the fallen leaves as I plodded toward the darkened theaters. It was a purposeless walk; I knew neither where I walked nor why, except to escape the presence of the juvenile villains behind me.

There was first the sound of an automobile, its engine roaring as the car drew abreast of me; then there was the sound of backfiring as the driver slowed the car suddenly, and a strange crackling in the air, or rather a whine or a zing. Only then did I consciously recognize the violent crack that was not an engine backfiring. Another one followed and I stepped with bewildered dignity behind the trunk of the nearest tree. Again the air seemed electrified and a bullet zinged afar off on a ricochet course. Yet another crack and the tree shuddered. The automobile roared; I heard the protesting screech of rubber and the car raced off.

Only then did I realize that I had been shot at. My stomach churned once, the beer boiling up my throat to burn my esophagus. My knees weakened and I leaned against the tree to save myself from falling. It was an enormity. New worlds suddenly opened before me; I realized how precious I was, how alive, how noble in aspect, how wonderful in all my parts. Only a fool would want to kill me.

But even that thought was too much to accept at the moment. Someone had shot at me, of that I had no doubt, but

I found it hard to believe that they, anyone, would want to *kill* me. Why, even during the *war* no one had wanted to kill *me.*

In sudden, overwhelming fear I pressed myself against the trunk of the elm. In time, I knew, I would come to think of my dignified retreat behind the tree as an act of consummate bravery, but at the moment I could only wonder how I could have been stupid enough to walk so slowly. Mentally I rehearsed the scene: this time at the first sound of the car I dived behind the tree, pulled from my holster a deadly Luger and shot twice. The first shot nearly drilled the driver of the car, the second killed the gunman; somehow it also punctured a tire and broke the engine.

The shots had raised no neighbors; no porch lights had flickered on as they had when I had so innocently broken the street lamp. I realized that I was in the industrial section of Stratford; the few blocks behind the theaters constituted the warehouse area, the *Pardonnez Moi* serving as the last outpost of industrialism before the residential district. Both sides of the street were lined with blind, brick walls; only the semibucolic nature of Stratford that admitted of occasional trees even in the warehouse district had saved me. And I blessed it unawares.

Again the point of the episode was driven home to me: someone had tried to *kill* me. My prejudices against the police vanished. I pushed off from the tree and broke into a dead run, heading straight for the Stratford Police station.

For the second time in as many nights I staggered breathlessly up the worn steps of the police building, stumbled down the corridor and shouldered open the door of Salter's office. Chief of detectives George Salter sat in his accustomed place behind the desk. I staggered to the chair before the desk, flopped and signaled for water.

"Couldn't you just drink at the public fountain the same as everyone else?" he said, but he waved to the shadowy, omnipresent Dan to bring me a drink from the wretchedly warm water cooler.

"Thumbs Brusick just tried to kill me," I said when I had caught my breath. Salter eyed me unequivocally; there was something a bit stronger than dislike in his steady gaze.

"I said he would; I can't quite bring myself to disapprove."

"That's a beastly attitude."

With great mock sadness he pulled the pad of yellow paper before him. "If you want to make a formal charge, go right ahead. But you had better have some proof that it was Thumbs Brusick."

"I have. He's the only one who *wants* to kill me."

"Want to lay a little side bet on that?" The dim light of his office, directed as it was on his desk, emphasized the darkness of Salter's skin and the jet blackness of his hair. His forehead was truly the smallest feature of his face. "Withers, you haven't called in three hours or more. I was just about ready to send Dan here out to scout you up. Not that we would have arrested you. I said it before, and I say it again, I will not have Brusick's mob fouling up my jail with your blood. I'll tell you what I'm going to do. I'm going to have Dan run you down to the depot. There's a milk train to Chicago due in here in about forty-five minutes. Dan will see that you get more or less safely on that train. But in any condition you will get on that train and get out of my district."

His attitude struck me as cavalier. He could apparently with impunity jail me or run me out of town on any charge that came to him at the moment.

"You mean, you're not going to hold me on the charge of murdering Downey?"

"I mean only that I want you out of town. If you ever show that foul beard in Stratford again, may heaven and the public defender protect you."

Obviously he didn't really suspect me of Downey's murder; what was more likely, he didn't suspect that Downey had been murdered at all. I wondered what he did know about the joint disappearances. It would be worth a lot to find out just what was concealed by that flattened cranium.

"You know very well," I began. "You know *damn* well that Brusick will learn about it if I go to Chicago. His thugs will run me down within half an hour after the train arrives."

"I don't know anything about anything that happens one-half mile outside of Stratford. But I'll read the *Tribune* carefully for the next few days in the hope that you're right." He nodded twice to emphasize that he was through with me and I felt Dan's meaty hand on my right shoulder. Roughly he turned me about and pushed me through the door.

Salter's car was parked at the back door.

Dan opened the door on the driver's side with his left hand and roughly shoved me in, following with his head and shoulders. I resisted him simply out of respect for my innocence; then I noticed that the keys were in the ignition

112

switch. It seemed worth a try. I stuck my left foot between the open door and the body of the car, then winced with mock pain.

"Look out! Ouch! My foot's caught."

Dan pulled back to examine the problem and I hit the ignition key with my right hand. As the engine turned over —for this was a well-kept automobile—I hit the transmission shift with the same hand. The car tugged backwards. I had shifted into reverse. Dan uttered a grunt and an oath as I kicked down the accelerator. The car bounded backwards; the swinging door shaved Dan neatly off his feet and left him sprawling face down in the alley. My left foot was still outside the car and before I could find the brake with my right foot, the car smashed violently into the assembled trash cans of the police station. Before I could stop the car several of these were crushed between the lacerated trunk of the car and the retaining wall at the end of the alley. I pulled into high gear and slipped my left foot in just as the forward motion swept the door closed.

The noise had been quite without precedent in Stratford; cans still shuddered and rolled behind me as the powerful car leapt forward and bore down on the painfully rising Dan. He saw the car and turned without bothering to assume an upright stance; like a great wallowing bear he scurried on all fours through the door of the station as I shot by him. I desperately swung the wheel and managed to negotiate the turn from the alley to the street.

I was away and free, but it struck me with some force that my actions hadn't been wise. What in the name of J. W.

Riley would I do? The car itself wasn't conspicuous, but I knew that Salter would be alerting police in Stratford and surrounding territory. I doubted that I had one chance in several trillion of driving away. And even if I made the odds, where would I drive to? Besides, the car was more conspicuous than it had been earlier in the evening. I was pretty sure that the rear end looked like a jet crash, and from the banging noise I half suspected that I dragged a trash can or two behind me.

Then I saw looming before me a cluster of dim lights that marked the train station at which I had disembarked so few hours before. It was the very depot that Salter had tried to send me to, and I realized that it was probably the last place — Linda Brusick's bed in the dormitory at Saint Felicitas always excepted — that Salter or Brusick would seek me. I slowed the car and pulled more or less quietly into the parking lot to the left of the station. There were perhaps seven cars parked in the lot, most of them soiled with rain and dust, indicating that the owners had parked their cars at the station while they wastrelled away a week or so visiting rich and decaying relatives. I pulled the car between two bespattered station wagons, turned out the lights and jumped ship.

The station was deserted, although noises indicated that someone in the baggage department was preparing for the arrival of the milk train. I chose a local paper from the news rack, kicked the stand to make the coins rattle, then chose a spot in the middle of the room.

Under the brightest light in the waiting room I sat, opened

114

the paper, spread it across my face and chest and prepared to sleep. As a last happy thought I removed my multi-heeled shoes, placed them on the bench behind my back, stretched out my weary legs, draped the paper across my beard and slept.

Chapter 6

I AWOKE IN A VILE TEMPER; my back hurt, my feet were cold and my head twice fell off onto the concrete floor as I tried to lace my shoes. In the cold and shallow light of the Stratford station, Bartie's beastly sofa took on the soft colorations of a houri's nest. How foolish I had been to complain of it. I had been awakened by the station agent's activities; he was preparing for the arrival of a train from some other godforsaken slum up or down the line. He paused momentarily in the midst of his meaningless busyness when I arose.

"Oh, good morning," he cried in unforgivable cheer. "I didn't see you come in. Train is due in just fifteen minutes." Whistling obscenely, he scuttled about behind his fumed oak counter.

I staggered back from the rest room a few minutes later, my face tingling from the cold water and harsh soap. I felt even worse than before because I had counted my money in the seclusion of the toilet and had found that my total assets, aside from my willingness to learn, were seven cents.

When I drew a balance on my human assets, it struck me that I was even worse off. There seemed hardly a soul in Stratford who didn't want to kill me. Bartie Barstairs didn't, of course, but his wife would stand by and smile mysteriously while I was drawn and quartered. Still, irrational antipathy wasn't so bad as intent to kill and I knew that I would come down upon the Barstairs like a wolf on the fold before that Sunday was long out.

"Well," said the foolish and evil station master when he saw that I had returned. "We had quite a time here last night. You should have been here."

The idea of murder was uppermost in my mind anyway and I sweetly contemplated the death of this grinning and whistling jackal. I would kill him and rifle the corpse for the three cents that I needed to make the ten cents that a telephone call to Bartie would cost.

"Listen, would you give me a penny for my thoughts?" I asked. "Or rather, three pennies?"

"You think I'm joking!" He threw back his head in a demented imitation of laughter. Sounds such as *Haw* and *Har* came from his twisted face. "This is no joke; we had great excitement here last night. Some guy stole the police chief's car and abandoned it here at the station. They think he took the three o'clock regular to Chicago or the four-fifteen flyer going south. I've been on the telegraph most of the night alerting station masters all along the line."

"How did they discover the car?"

"Well, actually, I found it. I saw this car in the parking lot, and its rear end was all banged in. Well, I thought, the

117

owner of that car simply has no pride, no self-respect at all, to let a beautiful car like that get so run down. Really, you can't imagine what it looked like — as though he had driven it into a pile of trash cans. Anyway, I was coming to work a few minutes early, as I always do, and I thought that I would just check the registration card to see whose car it was. You know, we're responsible for all the cars in the lot, responsible for everything but fire and theft of course, as the sign says. Well, you can imagine my surprise when I saw that the car was an official police car. . . . I called the police, and Chief of Detectives Salter himself came down."

I thought of my vulnerable position asleep in the center of the waiting room. "Did they search for the dirty crook?"

"Not here of course. I was in and out of this room a hundred times tonight, as every night, and I told them that there was nothing suspicious about *this* waiting room." He glanced at the clock behind him. "Excuse me, I have mail sorting to do before the train arrives."

He left the room and like a shot I dashed behind the counter and clawed at the cash drawer. The suspicious sod had locked the drawer before he left. I seized a handful of baggage tags and nipped around the counter again just as he appeared in the waiting room. If I had had sufficient money I would have boarded the first west-bound train, I think. I would have travelled straight to California and there have lived out my life on some lonely and deserted beach, eating driftwood and reading only messages washed ashore in bottles. I dared not attempt the trip without money. The trials and sorrows of the pioneers would have been as nothing to

118

three days locked in a railway jake. More than that, I felt a nagging desire to find out what did happen to old Jim Downey. And by then I was intrigued and puzzled by the conduct of that arch-Machiavel, Chief of Detectives George Salter. His conduct toward me had been beneath contempt; and his odd attitude toward the structure of the law had been barely praiseworthy. I wondered with a growing wonder how he had acquired the confidence to act as though he were the final arbiter of law in Stratford. Had the agencies of justice abdicated in his favor?

The pressing need, of course, was to get out of the station and to a place of relative security, if not of peace. My goal was Bartie Barstairs' home. My problem was how to achieve that goal without appearing on the naked Sunday streets of Stratford. My sole resources consisted of seven cents and a handful of baggage tags.

I scooped up the newspaper that had covered my face during the night and made my way back to the restroom. There I chose the booth nearest the track side of the station, opened the window so that I could hear the approaching train, and settled down to read. It was a boring interlude; the Stratford *Herald* was an incurious paper that retailed only local news. The editorials, on the other hand, were impassioned examinations of international policies. The classified ads, which I got around to reading before I heard the whistle of the morning train, were universal ones: dogs lost and cute houses for sale.

I waited at the door of the restroom until I heard the train come to a full stop. Waiting there I offered a prayer that I would not meet my cab driver of Thursday last; then I tore off the stubs of the baggage tags and dropped the stringed ends to the floor. As the hiss of escaping steam announced the halt of the train, I banged open the door, raced through the waiting room, burst through the main door and careened toward the cab stand. I wrenched open the door of the first cab in line and catapulted myself into the back seat. I also threw open the door on the other side and crouched ready to leap out again if the cab driver looked familiar. The first glance told me that he was a stranger, one I had never seen before. I clapped both doors to and settled back on the seat.

"Look, I don't have time to wait for my luggage," I said with earnest intensity. "Drive me to the Catholic church so that I can make Sunday Mass, then hop back here and collect my bags." I thrust the baggage stubs over his shoulder and onto his lap. The number of tags was impressive. "You can meet me at the church after Mass. And keep the meter running, I'm on travel expense."

The cabbie kicked over the engine but hesitated before engaging gears. I continued the confidence game. "I suppose you guys handle Diners Club cards?"

"Yah."

"Well, get rolling. Take me to the nearest Catholic church. No, wait a minute, is there a church near the college, Saint What'shername?"

"Yah."

"Well, go man." The taxi pulled away from the station. I felt that he wasn't quite convinced. "What time are Sunday Masses there?"

He shrugged. "Look, I won't even tell riders where the whoor houses are."

"Okay," I said and I relaxed against the cushion. At least his answer had justified me. That bugger deserved to be taught about justice and goodness.

The Catholic church proved to be less than five blocks from Bartie Barstairs'. It, too, was of red brick, its single ugly steeple pointed bluntly up into the bright autumn sky. The number of cars attested that Mass was in progress. As the taxi slowed, I leapt nimbly to the street, whispered intensely, "See you in half an hour with the bags," and dogtrotted briskly past the card table booth where chances could be purchased on a new Ford, past the card table booth selling Christmas cards of shocking taste, past the card table booth where tickets could be purchased for an approaching spaghetti dinner, up three steps and so into the church. Mass had begun; the sermon had just ended, as a matter of fact, and so I was after all fulfilling my Sunday obligation.

The church was filled but not crowded; an usher beckoned me toward the empty pews in the front of the church. I smiled winningly and limped a few steps forward to demonstrate to him that I had a stiff knee that allowed neither sitting nor kneeling. He smiled sympathetically and I limped painfully backward to the vestibule. I crossed myself and began to murmur from memory the prayers of the Mass. That was a process that automatically turned my mind into a freethought pattern, adrift among possibilities and dimly glimpsed probabilities. In times past I had found myself, during Mass, examining my past life, reviewing conversations of the previous evening, brooding over curricular changes, all the while I muttered the prayers of the Mass. *"Lavabo manus meas inter innocentes. . . ."*

This Sunday I pondered the problem of escape. If I were to wait until Mass ended the cabbie, empty-handed and angry, would surely be waiting for me outside the church. My height might allow me to escape disguised as an altar boy, but the beard would probably give me away. That wretched beard, straggly as it was, would give me away even if I tried to meld with a family group. But no more than my soiled and wrinkled clothes would. As I looked about the church at the scrubbed and groomed congregation, I realized that they were dressed, to a man, woman and child, in their starched, best clothes. Oh, well, I would wait out the Mass and see, *"Et ne nos inducas in tentationem, sed libera nos a malo. Amen."*

A full five minutes before the Mass was ended people began to hurry from the church. Their heads bent purposefully, they arose, genuflected gracelessly, and scurried away. In the vestibule I shifted out of their way, peering behind their retreating backs for signs of the taxi. The cab was parked at the curb and the cabbie was standing like the menacing figure that he was on the sidewalk in front of the church. As the priest left the altar the congregation turned and stampeded for the doors. For one moment of panic I feared that I would be swept before the mob and dropped on the sidewalk at the feet of my sullen enemy. Just in the nick of time I scooted into the last pew and knelt with my face buried in my hands as though in oblivious ecstasy.

When the church was nearly empty I arose and started toward the front of the church and the sacristy. My limp became more painful and more obvious as I approached the transept. I was barely able to drag my left leg as I passed through the communion railings. I did not bite my lips as if in pain, although I was tempted to do so. I had, however, thrown myself into the part of the noble and long-suffering cripple who had long ago given up lip-gnawing and had come to live at peace with his terrible and painful affliction. My limp was gross and, perhaps, not altogether convincing, for the usher emptying the collection baskets glared at me suspiciously. I returned his glare with a weary smile, one becoming a saintly man who had been crippled since birth.

I was not yet quite comfortable with the limp, and I had changed it from the left leg to the right and back to the left as I stumped down the center aisle of the church, but I felt confident that I had not been observed by this particular usher. In lieu of a genuflection I bowed profoundly toward the main altar and stumped into the sacristy.

The priest was divesting himself of the liturgical vestments. He was middle-aged and perhaps a bit more, but there was only a hint of grey in his close-cropped black hair. He was trim, athletic and perhaps nine inches taller than his humble servant.

"Are you the pastor?" I breathed piteously. He finished unvesting before he turned to me.

"Why, no," he said. "Saying Sunday Mass is only a hobby of mine. I'm really the housekeeper."

Two little signs flashed on in my head; one said, "Applause," and the other, "Look out for this one." I tried to obey both.

"I'm Red Withers, Father."

"Ah? Once before I was bothered by Chapped Thighs."

The door I was seeking was behind the priest; it led out of the sacristy, down a few steps and into a small driveway that opened into the alley. That way I could avoid the cabbie and could run by devious back ways to Bartie's. But there was still the possibility that Bartie would not be at home, and I resolved to hedge on that ill chance even though the knowing glint in the eyes of the priest was a warning.

"This is embarrassing for me, Father," I began, shifting painfully to my game foot, which seemed at the moment to be my left one. "I'm not a rich man." The priest, who had finished unvesting, clapped a biretta well forward on his head and faced me with arms folded. He offered no comment and so I continued humbly. "I intended to put a dollar bill into the collection box, but I find that I seem to have dropped a ten dollar bill by mistake. This *is* embarrassing, Father. I don't know quite how to say it, but I can ill afford to lose that much money."

"Well, at least that part of your story seems obvious," the priest said, then raised his voice to call the usher who was passing by the door behind me. "Oh, Charlie, will you fish one of the tens out of the collection baskets?"

"*One* of the tens? Father, have you lost your mind?"

"This fellow assures me that he dropped one in." I edged toward the outside door; it would be tricky getting by the priest. He was big.

124

"Hey, Father!" There was delight and amazement in the ancient usher's voice. "There *is* a ten dollar bill here." I settled back into my crooked stance.

"Of course," the priest and I said in unison.

"Thanks, Charlie. You can just leave the baskets here; I'll run them into the house in a bit. Thanks."

The usher tenderly dropped the basket onto the cabinet behind the priest and left us alone. The priest extended the crumpled bill. "Now, Mr. Withers, if you'll just hand me the dollar bill you originally intended to drop into the basket?"

Well, for all his size he was cute.

"That won't be necessary, Father. You can have the ten, of course. Perhaps you could just make up the change from the basket and give me nine ones. Or a five and four ones."

He shook his head in what could have been exasperated admiration, but he withdrew the money and fluttered it back into the basket.

"If brass were as costly as gold, you'd be a rich man, Mr. Withers. What is your real name, anyway?"

"It really is Withers."

"Does your foot pain you much?"

"It does now that I've been standing on my ankle for half an hour."

"Humph. Well, you wait here a few minutes while I say a thanksgiving prayer or two and then join me in the rectory for a cup of coffee. All right?"

"Righto, Father." If I could dawdle over that breakfast long enough the taxi would have left the church in despair.

125

The priest pushed by me and re-entered the sanctuary, where he knelt at a prie-dieu and cupped his face in his large and muscular hands. Only then did I realize that he had left me alone with the contents of the collection baskets. I felt like Jean Valjean, forced unwillingly to act the part of the good man. The literary parallel seemed apt. Anyway, I was sure of this: if there were sewers in Stratford some yahoo would be chasing me up and down their watery length before long.

When we were settled at the large oak table in the dining room of the rectory, after the bustling housekeeper had served the coffee and a platter of bacon and eggs, the priest addressed me.

"That trick you tried this morning, you know, is just about the oldest one in the world. It has an air of apostolic succession about it. Usually, though, it's the distraught wife of the parish alcoholic who tries it. What do you need the money for?"

"Well," I said, my mouth nearly filled with egg and bacon. "I drink a lot and gamble. Things like that."

"Humph. There are numerous operations on that poor foot of yours too, I suppose?"

"That's right, Father, and then I always try to tithe to the Baptist Church."

He pushed back from the table to rummage in the commodious pocket of his black cassock; soon he produced a dark and bitter looking pipe which he managed to light after it had given out a number of asthmatic gasps. He removed the pipe from his mouth, examined the fire, then nodded to me. "Well, you seem in all ways to be a most commendable young man. I wonder if you would care to address the Young Ladies' Sodality?"

"As a matter of fact, that's my vocation. I'm a professor at Saint Felicitas."

"Oh, come on, Withers." He arose from the table. "I think that I might believe any of the rest of it, but *this* is incredible." I stood too, but he silenced my complaint of honesty by saying a silent grace-after-meals. Standing or sitting, he gave the impression of immense strength.

"It's true, Father. I've been hired to serve out Jim Downey's contract." I had followed him into a bright, cheerful sun porch that overlooked a walled garden, now dry and crisp in the late autumn. He settled into a large, creaky wicker chair that groaned at his weight. To his left stood a table with ashtray, tobacco humidor and Chicago Sunday papers. On a card table under the uncurtained windows stood the Sunday collection baskets.

"Humph, I didn't know that Jim had left. Bit sudden, wasn't it?"

"Did you know him, Father?"

"Oh, yes. He was, if I'm any judge of character, your antithesis. Yes, knew him well. Sit down. For a minute." He underlined the time that I was expected to stay. I settled in an ancient wicker chair, the companion to his own. My feet barely touched the ground.

"Humph, and you say that your name is Withers?"

"Yes, Father, I'm afraid that I didn't catch yours."

"I'm Father Wallop, pastor here at Saint Perpetua and

127

apparently your host for the whole day." He paused to examine the pipe again. "Did you hear about that business of the school last night?"

I shook my head, thinking perhaps he had confounded the nights and really meant the Friday night fiasco in Downey's cottage. I would have liked to hear an objective report of that.

"A terrible and frightening thing in all ways," he continued slowly. "Of course we must be very careful not to judge. It's a matter for the Bishop anyway. For myself, I'm inclined to say it was temporary insanity. Humph. There's always the problem of scandal in these cases, though."

"What happened, Father?"

"One of the girls killed herself. As I said, we have to be careful not to judge suicide. Terrible thing."

"At school!" I was shocked. Suicide always seems such an alien thing, so distant and removed from one's own experience.

"Well, not at school. It was at a motel. The girl had apparently rented a room at a motel a couple of days ago and had locked herself in. It seems pretty certain that she was trying to cure herself of drug addiction. They called me in the middle of the night; as soon as the body was discovered. Those scenes are always terrible; and luckily — or perhaps unluckily — anyway, as luck would have it, the girl's father was in town."

"What was her name?"

"Brusick. Linda Brusick. Did you know her?"

"No, but I've been looking for her." I felt suddenly chill

and damp in that sunny room. It was all quite unreal: the old dark wicker, the rickety card table, the uncurtained windows, and the priest sitting across from me — all seemed unreal. And yet these tangibles, these visible things, were what I had known all my life. Either this priest and this rectory, or another quite like it. This was a part of my earliest life, and of my latest memory. Here things were easy to know, open to comprehension; here actions were understood if not judged, character was somehow intelligible and deeds meaningful. And yet all this seemed suddenly unreal. What was real was the world outside that window pane. Out *there* were such things as drug addiction, ugly men who hit and shot at me, policemen who shoved me rudely about. Out *there* was a broken and dented police car. All so strange and yet suddenly so real. And out there, beyond the sunny pane, in the dangerous dark, a girl had been driven to the ultimate madness.

"You didn't know her at all?" The priest was speaking. I shook my head. "Well, I arrived at the motel before the police did, brought the oils and all, but poor Linda was dead; had been dead for some time. The motel owner had been worrying about her and then when he saw the lights still on at that time of night he knocked on the door. Finally forced his way in. Terrible. She had slashed her wrists in the bathroom and then had walked in and lain down on the bed. He checked her identification; she had given a false name when she registered. Then he called the police and he called me.

"The leader of the police band around here is named

Salter. He's *not* a member of the parish, I might add. Anyway, he arrived a good deal later than I did. Something about his car; he wouldn't say, of course; he's so proud of that black monster. I'd bet that he simply couldn't get it started. Anyway, by the time that he arrived, Linda's father was there. Maybe you've heard of him. I remembered him from the Congressional investigations. Thumbs Brusick. A thoroughly bad one, I would guess, and that's hardly what would be called rash judgment. He was like a madman. What can you do in cases like that? A conditional anointing, say a prayer for the poor, dear thing, and hope that the Bishop views the case with charity. Brusick wanted to tear the place down. You wonder about grief like that . . . Oh, I suppose it's genuine enough. On one level he seemed close enough to the old-world traditions.

"If the fellow at the motel had called a doctor, it would have been easier on all of us; the doctor could have given Brusick a sedative of some kind. But the fellow had called the coroner. No doctor he; in Stratford we elect the coroner. We expect our coroners to have complete knowledge of the political party and the ability to distinguish between warm and cold. Humph."

"It's terrible of me to say this, I know. . . ."

"Tell me."

"I can't tell it in logical sequence; it's too real for that. But Thumbs Brusick thought that I was mixed up in a gang rumble that was responsible for his daughter's disappearance. He tried to kill me; three times last night, maybe four times, he shot at me. And the night before that his thugs beat me up. I've been hiding from them for days and that's why I tried to con you out of some money this morning. I *knew* that Linda's disappearance and Jim Downey's drop from sight were part of the same pattern, I. . . ."

"Whoa there, Withers. What's this to do with Jim?"

"This will probably surprise you, Father. . . ."

"There's little that will surprise a pastor after twenty years of hearing confessions."

"Well, Jim Downey . . ."

"What about Jim?"

"He took dope."

"No." We paused over that denial. I wiggled forward to place my feet firmly on the floor; he fiddled with his pipe and a blunt pipe tool.

"I've got proof, Father. Or at least, I had proof. I threw it away."

"Humph. I don't think that I'm breaking the seal of confession when I assure you that Jim is one of the best men I know. Now, *he* is one whom I *do* ask to lecture to the Sodality. No, Withers, no."

Another possibility occurred to me. "I haven't met him, so I don't know. But if he didn't take dope, he pushed it. He's a dope peddler."

"If it were true I'd hate to be in his shoes. Brusick is looking for the guy who hooked his daughter. But I *know* Jim. I'm his pastor and his friend. The whole idea is preposterous."

"But look, you know he disappeared with Linda?"

"I didn't know."

"Well, he did. The same night. Or no, that isn't right. Carol said it was the day after Linda disappeared that he disappeared. Anyway they both had hypodermic kits, dope kits. I found them."

"I don't know what you found, but I know that Jim is a good boy. He and I play chess together on Tuesday evenings when he doesn't have class. Your talk of dope peddling is utterly absurd, Withers. I don't know what you're trying to prove."

"For the past few days I've been trying to prove that Downey and Linda ran off together." Father Wallop snorted at that. "Because that was the only way I knew that I could prove to Detective Salter that I didn't kill Downey to get his job; and I had to prove to Brusick that I didn't abduct his daughter. Really, both of those ideas strike me now — as they did at the very first — as nutty explanations of a very simple situation. But those harebrained ideas almost killed me. This is one wild little town."

"Ah, I know. Are you sure that it was Brusick who shot at you last night?"

"Oh sure. Or one of his gang." I paused a moment to reflect on that. "Well, I'm not sure of course. It might have been that punk from *Pardonnez Moi*. I wonder if he could have followed me?"

"So you know of that place, *Pardonnez Moi?*"

"I do, Father. Do you?"

"There's little I don't know about Stratford. I know, for instance, that narcotics are a good deal more plentiful than most people would believe. I suppose all vice is a good deal more plentiful than most people would allow themselves to believe. There's drunkenness and a wild sort of gambling and prostitution here, but I fear you find those most places. Drugs, though. It seems to me that there's been a terrible increase in drug traffic here of late. And it's the kids, of course, who suffer."

"Did you ever talk to Downey about this?"

"It would be like lecturing the First Communion Class on the dangers of adultery. Hush now with talk about Jim Downey being involved with drugs. It isn't so."

"There's one more possibility, Father. Do you think he could have been an undercover agent, you know, working for the FBI to uncover the pushers?"

"He has no guile about him, no deception at all."

"But I found a heroin kit in *his* medicine chest."

"Are you sure now? It couldn't have been a diabetic's equipment? But then Jim isn't diabetic anyway. Humph."

"No, it was a kit all right. I destroyed it, foolishly I suppose."

We sat in silence for a while. I was contented at least on the most basic level, having eaten the first pleasant breakfast I had for months and months and months. But the talk of vice had recalled my own failings and I felt a growing thirst for a stomach-settling glass of beer. The Sunday-selling laws of Stratford were strange to me and in any event I was reluctant to leave the priest's rectory.

"Well, what are you going to do?" he asked.

I was taken aback for a moment until I realized that his mind moved to larger issues than did mine.

"Do?" I croaked as dryly as I could.

"Humph."

"Well, I don't know." And I didn't. It had come to me that Sunday-selling laws were of no importance to me unless I could come into some money. Anyway, the priest was not talking about ways of cadging a beer, but about a course of conduct. "I really do have a job at Saint Felicitas, but Detective Salter has a score to settle."

"Ah, Withers, Withers, are you the true confidence man? Do you think only of yourself? I meant, what do you plan to do about Jim's disappearance. If it *was* a drug addict's equipment that you discovered in his medicine chest — and what were you doing in there anyway? — shouldn't you notify the proper authorities?"

"You mean, Salter?"

"Yes, I suppose he's the one."

"But I threw the thing away to protect Downey's name."

"Grief, man, he doesn't need that kind of aid from you. But even if he were guilty, even if he were, shouldn't the police be told? Shall I tell you just how prevalent narcotics have become in Stratford? Do you know that no one is ever really cured of addiction to heroin? Do you want a word picture of Linda Brusick's motel room? Oh, yes, Salter's a small town cop and he has what I suppose are all the failings of his type. But he has a suicide and a disappearance on his hands now, and we should give him all the help that we can."

"Okay, Father, okay. I'll tell him, if I can do it on the telephone. I surely don't want to meet him."

134

The priest indicated a phone in a corner of the sun porch. "Do you think he'll be at the police station now?"

"You can try."

"Is there an extension? You can listen, Father; this ought to be good for a couple of laughs." He nodded, heaved himself from the wicker chair and made for the rear of the rectory. I dialed the police number. After several rings Salter himself answered.

"Hallo?"

"This is the Epitome Body and Fender Repair Shop; we'd like to offer an estimate on your car. We can make the rear end look as good as new again. . . ."

"Withers?" he shouted.

"Or for just a few dollars more we can make the whole body match the rear end."

"Withers, I'm having this call traced. In a matter of minutes you will be encircled by my police cars. It will go easier on you if you tell me where you are."

"*Beep*," I said. "I don't think that you have *Beep* the equipment to trace calls. *Beep*. Listen, are you *Beep* making a recording of this call? Because *Beep* you'll have to clear any recording rights *Beep* with the Public Relations Office at Saint Felicitas." There was a silence for some seconds. "*Beep*," I said.

"Just keep it up, Withers. I'm tracing the call right now." I felt pretty sure it was bluff. I wished fervently that I knew more about the dial telephone system. At the very worst I might be able to claim sanctuary in the church. "Give yourself up, Withers."

"*Beep*. Listen, I know something about Jim Downey. He had a narcotics kit in his possession. I found it in the medicine chest in his cottage on campus."

There was silence. Was he still trying to bluff, or was the phone call being traced? I tried to match him in patience but failed quite clearly. After only a few seconds I knew that I simply had to hang up. "Well, *Beep* I guess that's all I have to say. The weather's fine here; rain, but a fine rain."

"Withers!" There was metal in the sound. "Withers, I'm formally charging you with the murder of Jim Downey. Any further effort to evade me will be construed as attempts to escape justice. Now, where are you?"

"*Beep*," I said, "this has been a recorded transcription." And I hung up.

"Now what was all that about his car?" said Father Wallop as he came back into the sun porch.

"Would you believe it if I told you that I drove it into a pile of trash cans when I was escaping from jail?"

"Yes," he said.

"Oh? Well, would you believe me if I told you I didn't know anything about his old car?"

"No."

"Well, then, let me show you what happened. You don't happen to have a couple of toy automobiles about, do you? I could demonstrate on the table top here. No? No little cars? Oh well, two beer cans will do as well."

The priest shook his head. "You're incorrigible."

"Father Flanagan used to say to me, 'There's no such thing as a bad boy. Withered, yes, but not bad.'"

"Father Flanagan was an idealist; my housekeeper is something else and she would consider me debauched if I ordered a beer for you at this time of the morning." He settled back into the wicker chair. "Now tell me what you know about Jim. Tell everything."

"Really, I've already told you everything I know. He taught at Saint Felicitas; he wears my size in pajamas, almost. He had a drug outfit in his medicine chest, and he seems to have disappeared."

"Humph. Then why does Salter think that you killed him?"

"I don't think he does. I mean, that was the third time he *accused* me of killing Downey. But twice he simply let me go. You think he would have taken a fingerprint or something. Booked me, anyway. That charge of murder is just a stick to stir me."

"Well, I confess that I can't understand this. Jim Downey is a very fine boy. It seems ridiculous to speak about a lad like that in terms of murder. But I can't believe that he would just walk out of his responsibility at the college either. He was very sincere about his teaching career. I wonder if there could have been an accident."

"Wouldn't Salter know about an accident?"

"I suppose he would. Now let me remember. . . . Humph, the only other friend that Jim has, as far as I can recall, was that Barstairs fellow. He's a member of the parish. I wonder if he would know?"

"He's the guy who invited me down here. He didn't know anything the last time that I talked to him, but I could call him again."

"Why don't you do just that. And, and, humph, I'll just explain to the housekeeper who the pastor is. That's a point I should make more often anyway. Will you have the beer in the can or a glass?"

"A saucer will do nicely, Father."

There was again a great groaning and grinding of wicker as we both arose; he made for the kitchen and I picked up the telephone directory.

Bartie answered the phone in a breathless whisper. "Hullo?"

"Bartie? This is Red. How is What'shername, Mary?"

"She's resting now. I thought she better stay in bed again. I'm having her read my old Hugh Walpole novels now. I think they should put her to sleep. Say, isn't it fine about Linda and Jim? I mean, they didn't run off the way you said at all."

"I think that's shocking, Bart." And I was shocked. I was surprised that I could say it though, surprised that I wasn't as speechless as I suddenly felt. It was appalling that Bartie should welcome Linda's suicide simply because it meant that his friend had not been involved in an elopement and a common-law marriage. It was some seconds before I could attend to what he was saying.

"So I guess you haven't heard about it, but Linda called here late last night, well, it was this morning really." He chuckled mechanically. "When the telephone rang, it woke Mary and she thought it was you. She stopped this side of hysterics though, and I was proud of her. I mean, it's hard on the child but he's probably learning stamina from Mary.

Anyway, as it turned out it wasn't you at all. It was Linda Brusick. She was asking for Jim. Of course he wasn't here, but that means that they didn't run off together. I told her I didn't know where he was, didn't have any idea really, and she rang off. But at least they didn't elope. Did they? Red? Red?"

I dropped the telephone into its cradle and leaned heavily on the table. In a few moments the priest came back carrying a beer can and a bottle of ginger ale. He offered the beer to me.

"What is it at all?"

"Linda called Bartie asking for Jim, apparently just a little while before she slashed her wrists." I remembered the telephone call for Downey that I had sleepily taken late Thursday night — the night I had slept at Bartie's. If that was Linda, she must have already been *in extremis,* attempting drug withdrawal on her own; and if she called for Downey in that state, I could assume that she called him because he knew something about it. She wouldn't report herself to an innocent party. She was calling someone who already knew something of her plight — if it was Linda.

"Then there was something between them," the priest said.

"I know that they both had narcotic kits. At least they had that in common. I know that they had *that* in common; I don't care what you think about him."

He stared out the window at the autumn garden for the space of a moment, or until I had seized the can and had drunk the first long gulp. "There are a few things about you that still puzzle me, Withers. I gather that you are a fugitive from Salter *and* from Brusick. I'd like to know just which one of them drove you into the sacristy this morning."

"I can easily explain."

"Oh, I have no doubt of *that*. I'm sure you can present an adequate explanation, but never mind. It would seem that Brusick has lost interest in you. You obviously weren't involved in his daughter's death. Salter surely doesn't know where you are. And yet you did seem a hunted man, a man closely pursued, when you popped in on me after Mass."

"I was. For one thing, I didn't know about Linda's death; and for another, there are two other guys in Stratford who are hunting for me."

"Sometimes the line between the guilty and the innocent is hard to draw. Sometimes it seems that the injured has done all that he can to provoke his attacker. And when the race is close, who can tell the pursuer from the pursued?" He paused to knock his pipe against the ashtray. "I think that an example of a truly unprovoked crime would be difficult to find. But you, Withers, might well be the exception. I don't know if I would be surprised to find in your past a trail of injured widows and children. You *look* guilty."

"That's just because I'm short. I had a pair of elevator shoes once that made me look like a pillar of the community."

"Humph. Well, we might be able to put that guilty look to some good use. Tell me now, do you want to stay in Stratford?"

"I suppose. I don't really know. I have a job here, at least a temporary one, and how my account stands in Chicago it's hard to tell."

"And do you think that narcotics had something to do with Jim's disappearance?"

"You know him, Father. I don't, but there doesn't seem to be any other explanation."

"The good Lord knows I'd like to get my hands on the people who are selling the stuff in Stratford. Let me make a bargain with you. If you'll find the seller of the drugs, the pusher, using your evil looks and what I have no doubt is sufficient knowledge of the underworld — if you find the pusher who might know something about Jim's disappearance, I'll put in a word for you with Salter to make it possible for you to stay on here at the college."

I agreed. For one thing I knew that Downey had become too much a part of me in the past two days to allow me to walk away from Stratford with careless heart. I suppose I would have struck upon some such plan on my own, but the priest's offer seemed a good one. In time I reasoned that I had suggested the plan to him with my talk of Downey acting as an undercover agent. At the moment the idea of working on the side of order and justice appealed strongly.

We decided that I should stay in the rectory, on the day bed in the basement if I chose, until Monday. There seemed little opportunity to seek out a dope peddler during the somnolent daze of a Stratford Sunday.

Together Father Wallop and I read the Sunday papers. The Stratford paper, of course, had been printed too early to carry the news of Linda's death. It occurred to me as I sucked on the empty beer can and brooded over the Sunday funnies that the news of her suicide would put the dope pusher or pushers on their guard.

"Do you think, Father, that there is any chance of suppressing the announcement of her death for a day? It would make my job a lot easier."

"We can try, I suppose." The priest picked up the telephone and dialed 116. "Hello, Father Wallop here. Would you just connect me with Chief of Detectives Salter? Oh, is that you, Dan? Fine, thanks. . . . Good for you and how's the wife? . . . Good, good. . . . Yes, if you'll just put him on. George? Father Wallop here. . . . Fine, thanks. Did you get any sleep yourself last night? I wonder if perhaps you would do me a favor, George? . . . Well, I know you would, thank you. This is about Linda. Do you think that we could perhaps keep the information from the newspaper for a day? It's for a good reason but I'd rather not go into it now. . . . Ah? Well, many thanks, George." Father Wallop turned to me.

"Too late, I'm afraid. They took her to the mortuary instead of the morgue. Half the old ladies in Stratford must know about it already."

When we had finished the papers, the priest settled down to deal with his Sunday collection and I retired to the day couch in the basement. The bed proved to be in a class with Bartie's sofa. Perhaps Father Wallop slept there as a Lenten penance. I'm sure that the restless hour I spend writhing on its corrugated mattress did oceans of good for my soul. In time I crept upstairs; all was quiet in the rectory. Father Wallop was apparently taking an afternoon nap.

In the bathroom I inspected his medicine chest; there was no evidence of drug addiction there of course, but the paucity of bottles bespoke a reprehensible lack of hospitality. There were neither deodorants nor aspirins, neither shaving lotion nor cologne. The shaving soap was a bar of Ivory; the shaving brush stiff and balding, the razor old and unsanitary looking. With some reluctance I shaved my cheeks, levelling the side burns. I was forced to comb my hair and beard with my fingers. More and more I was beginning to look like an accident. Nevertheless I slipped out the back door of the rectory and skulked through alleys toward the college. I thought to begin my search for the dope pusher with Linda's roommate. Perhaps confronted with the horror of Linda's death, Carol O'Connor would recall something that would serve as a clue.

It was visiting Sunday on the campus. Elderly couples strolled about the campus beaming shyly at the embarrassed daughters who reluctantly walked a few steps in front of them. A gaudily bedaubed "Welcome Mom and Dad" sign was stuck in the lawn a few paces from the front door of the dormitory. Within, there was enough bustle to make my progress up the stairs unnoticed. On the second floor most of the doors stood open. "Saint Ethelreda's" seemed to contain a wild Italian reunion. In "Saint Brigid" a girl laughed mirthlessly at her father who stood holding a book in either hand.

Carol's door was closed and a hotel sign for *Quiet Please*

hung from the doorknob. I opened the door and slipped in. Carol lay curled on the bed. She was wrapped in the trench coat in which I had first seen her. Her eyes were open but she made no move to see who had entered her room. I closed the door and stepped into her line of vision. She spoke but did not move. The chestnut hair was now unkempt.

"What do you want?"

"Hello, Carol. . . . Have you heard?"

"About Linda? Yes, *they* haven't." She indicated the parents and the students with an impatient sweep of her arm. She sat up then, hugged the coat about her and swung her legs over the side of the bed. "Give us a cigarette?"

I withdrew one from the opened pack on her desk, lit it, and handed it to her along with the nearly filled ashtray that I found there.

"Im sorry, Carol."

"Sure, sure. Everybody's sorry for poor old Carol." She twitched the coat to make a lap for the ash tray. "My folks are going to come tomorrow and take me home." With the heel of her right hand she dug savagely at her tear-rimmed eyes.

"I am sorry. I thought perhaps that you might have remembered something, a clue, or a name or something. Anything that might tell where Linda got her drugs."

"No, I told you no. I don't know. How should I know? Do you think I'd lie? Oh well, never mind, I haven't any idea."

"Do you think it was at *Pardonnez Moi?*"

"I don't know. I don't know. She went there a lot, but she had the stuff sometimes even when she wasn't going

144

there regularly. I don't know; maybe once she said something about the Canary."

"The Canary?"

"I don't know what it means; I just happened to think about it now. I don't remember really."

I glanced about the disorderly room; there was some evidence of packing. Suitcases were piled before the door of the cluttered closet. Two unequal stacks of books were placed in the center of the far desk. A pile of rumpled small clothes still occupied the chair.

"Have you gone through Linda's things?"

"I suppose so; I started to anyway, but then I started to cry. I loved Linda, I really did. Do you know what it means that she killed herself? To a Catholic it means that she goes to hell."

"Oh, stop it. It does not. Don't you judge Linda just to give yourself an easy cry. You're feeling sorry for yourself."

"I am not!" Carol shot to her feet, spilling the ashtray and ashes onto the floor. It was easy to see how the room came into such disorder. "And you get out of here, whoever you are." I was fingering through the clutter on the desk and I did not look at her stiff figure.

"Look, you're distressed and upset, but it would be unnatural if you weren't. I'm the professional student is who I am, and I know an awful lot about college roommates. I don't think there's any relationship so close and intimate except that of a long and bitterly argued-out marriage. You can't live so intimately with a person day in and day out without coming to love or to hate. You loved Linda and I'm

145

sure she loved you, but don't parade your distress. Linda deserves better than that."

She shivered in the coat and looked about her. "What will I do?"

"Just answer some questions for now; perhaps you can do more later."

"I go home tomorrow. My parents really are coming for me."

"Okay, then just answer the questions. Does the college know about Linda?"

"The Sisters do; the girls don't."

"Do they know about Linda's addiction?"

"I didn't tell anyone. After you left yesterday I threw the kit down the incinerator shaft, so there's no evidence."

"No evidence at all? Are you sure? I mean, you haven't gone through all of Linda's things yet."

"No, but Linda was terribly secretive the last month or so. Maybe months ago she might have left a clue; this last month she hid everything, everything but that one little razor kit. It wasn't so much that she feared being caught, you know. I think she was really hiding the evidence from herself. Anyway, for a month or so dope wasn't a game anymore. She wouldn't let me talk about it, and I never saw her take any. She used to have, you know, marijuana, a couple of different kinds of needles, even books on it. But they all disappeared; she got rid of them all."

"And you haven't any idea where she got the dope?"

"No." Carol drooped at the desk.

"What about the Canary?"

146

"Oh, that. I don't know; it just occurred to me. Linda used to say, you know once in a while, she would say, 'I'm going to see a canary about a horse.' "

"So it had something to do with narcotics?"

"I suppose." Carol yawned and fumbled with the cigarette pack. "Suddenly I feel real weird. Sister Ransom gave me some sleeping pills just before you came."

She rose unsteadily and groped in the pocket of her coat. "She said I should take two more pills if I wasn't sleepy in a few minutes." She produced a white envelope by then, but seemed too weary even to stand.

I took the pills from her limp hand, dropped them into the pocket of my jacket and steered her to the rumpled bed.

"Oh golly," she said and dropped sleepily face downward. By the time I had reached the door her heavy breathing had taken on the faint hint of a snore.

Swiftly I beat my way back to the rectory of Saint Perpetua's. The first glance at Father Wallop's day-pallet resolved the doubt in my mind; I swallowed the sleeping pills — there proved to be four of them and great red boluses they were — settled myself on the corrugated mattress and slept.

Chapter 7

THE HEAVY HAND of the priest awoke me to a day that proved to be one of my most memorable. Only two days remain firmly fixed in my mind in all their incandescent color: on one of those days I arrived penniless, hopeless and beardless at the American embassy in Rome and found my delayed Fulbright check; on the other day, the day that began with the meaty sacerdotal hand on my shoulder, I was shot at and hit. A day of bright, springtime sunshine will bring the first day back to me with all the splendor of gay and gaudy Rome; a damp and showery day will, on the other hand, bring a twinge to my left shoulder and remind me of the bullet scars I still bear.

Father Wallop and I shared a sullen breakfast; he was immersed in the Stratford newspaper that retailed the death of Linda Brusick. I brooded over my coffee and waited with bad grace for him to relinquish the paper. When he had digested the paper apparently down to the last item on the

148

sports page, he folded it, drained his coffee cup and looked at me with mock surprise.

"Hallo, you still here?"

"Yes," I said. Well, it wasn't a clever rejoinder but what could I have said? "I was waiting for the paper."

"Nothing in it to interest you, I'm sure. All local news."

"What does it say about Linda? May I see?"

"You'd do better out on the streets looking for the dope peddler. The paper says nothing new. There's to be a coroner's inquest on Linda's death tomorrow. I suppose that means they will call me, but there's nothing here that you don't know." He arose and said a silent grace. He tucked the paper under his arm and made for the door; at the threshold he turned back. "I suppose you'll be gone when I come back? Well, luck."

"Wait a minute, Father. If I find the pusher, will you square everything with Salter so that I can stay here? The car business too?"

"What is it about the car?"

"Never mind what about it; will you square things?"

"Withers, or whatever your name is, if you put the finger on the dope traffic in Stratford, I'll see to it that you become *persona grata*."

"Do you think that Downey was responsible for Linda's death?"

"Obviously not. I don't know what has happened to Jim, but I *know* he hasn't done anything wrong. It's just not in him."

"I suppose you know."

"I do." He turned back toward the door and the bowels of the rectory as I called after him.

"May I use the phone before I start out?" I took his silence for consent. In the sun parlor I looked up Bartie's telephone number again and called him.

"Hello, Bartie? Red here."

"Red! Have you seen this morning's paper?"

"No, but I know about Linda's death. Is that what you mean?"

"Of course. Imagine what this would do to Mary! I've burned the paper already."

"I think that was probably wise of you. Listen, Bartie, I called to ask about classes. Do I have any classes today?"

"Well, of course; Monday is a very heavy day."

"I want to keep that position at Saint Felicitas, but I can't make classes today."

"No?"

"No, and don't inflect your voice like that."

"Well, I mean, Red old boy, I did practically sponsor you at college. How will it look if you don't show up for classes the first day?"

"It can't be helped. Will you tell Sister Mary Ransom that I went back to Chicago for my clothes and that I was delayed by the strike? Tell her I'll be there for classes, God willing, tomorrow."

"What strike?" Bartie asked suspiciously.

"How do I know what strike? I haven't seen the papers this morning. There's always a strike on somewhere. Just tell her that *the* strike kept me, but that I'll be there for classes tomorrow."

150

"I don't think that Downey had any classes on Tuesday. Anyway, I don't. On Tuesday Mary and I go for long walks."

"Well, Wednesday then, okay?"

"I don't know, Red. I hate to tell lies to a nun. To anyone for that matter."

"You don't have to tell a lie. Just tell her that I called and *said* that the strike held me up. That's the truth." I waited while he measured this against his conscience. It was exasperating. While talking to him I was trying to plan a method of attack. How would I go about finding a dope pusher in Stratford? Whom would I ask? Where would I go? Where would I start? I had no idea at all. Should I start at the least probable point on the assumption that any one was good as another? "Oh forget it, Bartie. Never mind."

"No, I'll say that much, that you called and said something about a strike."

"Look, where can I buy narcotics?" My question met with silence, save for the indefinable quality that marks a live connection. That vital silence now changed from a shocked silence to a prim silence, but still Bartie didn't answer. "Bartie? Did you hear me?"

"Yes?" Very prim; it was a mew really.

"Well, do you know?"

"Mary just walked into the room . . . Hello, dear."

"Ask her where I can get a bop."

"Really, Red."

"Okay, okay, just tell me this: is her doctor O.G. or a general practitioner?"

"He's a G.P., Doctor Adjello, but I know that he won't, won't . . . well, never mind. . . . It's just Red, dear. . . . Yes,

I know. . . . No, he didn't. . . ." His voice faded then, was blotted out as he apparently cupped his hand over the mouth piece of the telephone. I hung up.

On the front porch of the rectory I glanced up and down the street. On the assumption that Linda's demise had scratched me from Thumbs' list, and on the assumption that Salter's black, unmarked limousine was in the body repair shop, I had only to be on the lookout for marked cars: either black and white police cars or yellow taxi cabs. Otherwise I was a pretty free agent in Stratford.

I started walking toward town, down streets that were growing daily more familiar. Monday was washday in Stratford. The men were in the counting houses, the children in school, and the women in cellar or backyard hanging up the clothes. The streets and sidewalks were deserted. At each intersection I paused and looked to my left and to my right. At one corner I saw what I was looking for: two blocks to my left there was a corner drug store. Toward the dim and faded sign DRUGS-SUNDRIES I made my way.

The windows of the store were clotted with water-stained cardboard posters that advertised patent medicines. To the left of the dark and rusty screen door a large tin thermometer registered the temperature and suggested that I buy aspirin. Within, the store was musty. A brown tile soda fountain stretched along the left wall, tall and backless wire stools were arranged before the counter. To my right was the hideously bright array of cheap magazines. Waist-high gondolas in the middle of the room displayed school supplies, penny candies and gift packages of notorious cosmetics. As I approached the ancient proprietor, who was arranging flashlights into a display that would resist selling, it occurred to me that I still didn't have any money.

"Good morning," he said flatly as I approached.

"Not for me, it isn't. What do you have for the shakes?"

"Bromo? Bromo'd probably do just fine."

"No. I got shakes worse than that." I steadied myself against the wooden partition of his prescription department. "I've got cramps, too, that I can't stand much longer."

"Sounds like you need something more laxative than a Bromo." I opened my eyes as wide as I could and stared about the store, avoiding his glance as my bugging eyes swept past him.

"I've got to have something. I know you don't sell drugs, not the kind I need, but I've got to have some. Look, I'm just passing through town; by this evening I'll be back in Chicago. I'm under the care of a physician there. They let me come down on this trip only for my mother's funeral, and I had just enough stuff to last until I got back there and under treatment again. Only the strike held me up and it's all gone now, and look, if it's money or a doctor's prescription — I can get that for you tomorrow. I'll mail it." I refocused my eyes and turned on him a pathetic stare.

"Get out," the old bugger said.

"Well, if you'll just tell me where . . . only enough for now."

"Get out. I don't keep any narcotics here just because I don't want any truck with people like you. Customer wants a prescription filled that calls for something like that I send him downtown. You go right on down there and get arrested, but get out of here."

"But there must be some way. . . ."

"Get out."

The old grouch was actually fumbling with one of the flashlights as though he were planning to attack me with it. I retreated before he could whip himself into a state. I paused in my flight only long enough to scoop up the few dimes atop the pile of morning papers at the magazine rack. It was a contradiction for a man who had so little trust in me to leave money lying about as a temptation.

I spent the money for coffee at a number of cafes near the Stratford consolidated high school. At each place I nursed my cup between shaking hands. I drained the color from my face and tore the napkins to shreds. The proprietors were sympathetic but unhelpful. Either they were bewildered by my pleas for "real help" or they were consummate masters of disguise. The trail of Bromo was clear; I picked it up at the first stop and found it again each time I tried to simulate withdrawal symptoms. But there was no evidence of traffic in narcotics.

Was the sale of narcotics as much a part of the pattern of life in Stratford as Father Wallop suggested, or had he exaggerated to engage my free services? I felt nothing of the crusader in me, but I was beginning to detect a hint of the patsy.

Only once during the exhausting day did I have a brush with the law. I had entered a drug store in the semi-industrial part of the town, close to the river area. The store showed evidence of prosperity out of keeping with the merchandise displayed. The shelves were for the most part barren; the soda fountain was stained, sticky and unused.

But new fluorescent lights illumined the farthest reaches of the store and a shiny new tile graced its well-used floor. The druggist was young, antiseptic looking, and vigorous. I tried a frontal attack; that is, there was deceit in my approach but little obliquity. I met the drugger bluntly.

"You don't know me, of course. I'm driving my wife from a rest home in Evanston to a sanitorium outside Ashville. To be frank with you, she has a monkey on her back. She needs a kicker now; whatever you can spare. I can pay but I need the stuff immediately."

He eyed me steadily for one brief moment. "Certainly, sir. Heroin? How much?"

"You mean, how much can I pay? Well, you've got me there. You know how badly she needs it."

"No, no sir. We can settle that. I meant, how much do you need?" He smiled winningly. I noticed that he had enormous ears, parentheses to a quite fatuous smile.

"Well, I'm afraid she'll need a big one. It's a long ride ahead."

"If you'll just wait a moment." He nodded to the fixed stools by the fountain and retreated to the back of the store.

It was the barrenness of the shelves I suppose, or the slick surface of the new floor, that made an amplifier of that store. As I settled onto the sticky stool I heard the idiot dialing the phone. Was he calling the pusher? The clicking of the dial stopped too soon for that. I strained to hear: click . . . zip, click . . . zip, clickickickck. No more. Only three numbers? Damn, *I* knew who had a three-digit telephone number in Stratford. I shoved from the stool and raced for the back of the store. The druggist was crouched over the telephone in the attitude of a scout blowing a minute ember into the start of a campfire. He was breathlessly wrapt, oblivious of my entry; when I clapped him on the shoulder he whirled and emitted a purely animal sound of fear. I smiled encouragingly and plucked the telephone from his nerveless hand.

"Good boy," I said and his ears quivered. Then I spoke into the telephone. "Hello, Salter?"

"No. Operations. Do you want Chief of Detectives Salter?"

"Belcher here. I told you this place was clean."

"What?" the crude and rasping voice of Operations showed some annoyance.

"Do you know who that was that put the call in?" I smiled winningly at Pitcherears. "Sure, he was going to report me."

"Is this a gag?" snarled Operations.

"Next time you send me out on an undercover job, have better evidence than the report of an old lady."

"This call," said Operations, with a feeble effort to control his rising anger, "is tantamount to a false alarm. It can be construed as a felony."

I chuckled. "Sure, I'll apologize for you." I replaced the receiver in its cradle and turned to my young, numb companion. "Chief of Detectives Salter said that he would drop you a note of commendation. I might add on my own that your conduct was superb. It's always difficult to explain these investigations — how they begin and all. Well, do you know Old Lady Fish?"

"Who doesn't?"

"Well, enough said then." I extended my hand in a suddenly frank gesture of camaraderie. "Bless you, son."

"Thank you, Detective Belcher." His ears reddened alarmingly. It must have drained whole arteries so to color those flanges. I shrugged and strolled from the store, netting another four dimes from the newspaper rack.

It was only a few blocks to the bar that I had visited Friday evening when flushed with success and wealth. Thither I directed my halting steps; one of my many heels had again worked its way loose.

The change from the late afternoon light to the stygian gloom of the bar was abrupt. It was a moment or more before I could detect the lighted beer advertisements. The bar seemed empty; in the heavy gloom at the rear something moved; before I could make out the bartender I heard him.

"You stay the hell out of the phone booth this afternoon."

"I wouldn't go in there on a bet; the place smells. Besides, the telephone doesn't flush." I put three of my dimes on the counter. "If I'm drunk by the time all this is used up, you just throw me out. Start setting them up now."

"You want a beer?" he asked, coming behind the bar.

"Yeh, just bring the whole bottle." I noted that he scooped up the money before he brought the bottle and glass. I poured and drank thirstily. "I guess you know why us guys are down here," I said as a conversational starter. My remark met with silence. Not only did the bartender not know what I was talking about; it was clear he couldn't think of anything to say. "Thumbs Brusick and us guys come down here over the week end."

"Yah?" There was excitement in his voice. "I heard about it all on the radio." From the beginning of our relationship I had known that he couldn't read, but I was moderately pleased to learn that he had taught himself to tune the radio.

"Yah, some of us guys who were in here Friday night think you're okay. The guys who were here when I come in, they say you're okay. So you're okay."

"You guys are all okay too. You drink that, the next one is on the house. Thumbs Brusick, eh? He must be an okay guy."

I was beginning to find it a strain to converse with only a dozen words.

"Thumbs Brusick is okay," I said. I marvelled that missionaries to the South Pacific were reported to have made converts using only Basic English. "You think I'm okay?" I challenged.

"You're okay," he said.

"In Chicago I got connections. I can get things done. And I can *get* things, know what I mean?"

"Go on." He leaned his elbows on the bar and bent attentively forward.

"I need a fix; almost anything will do. In Chicago all I have to do, I make a telephone call and zip, there the stuff is."

"Just like that, huh?"

"Zip." I emphasized the point by swilling his beer. "In this town I don't know where to go, so I come to the one guy which I know he is okay."

"What do you want?"

"I need the real stuff. Thumbs don't care."

"He don't?"

"Nah. Of course he's all broke up over his girl. You read about that?" The bartender nodded; he was flattered. "Well, he says to me, 'get something to steady yourself; I'm going to need your strength now.'"

"He said that, huh?"

"So where can I get some strength?"

"I wish I could help you. It'd just be like helping Thumbs hisself."

"You don't know?" My hopes were dashed.

"I don't know nothing. Oh, there's plenty of the stuff around, but it's kind of a monopoly, know what I mean?"

"But you don't know who runs it?"

"I don't know. Why don't you ask a cop?"

"You joke."

"I mean, you find an okay cop maybe and have Thumbs talk to him, you know, one okay guy to another okay guy."

"You know an okay cop?"

"I wish I did."

"But you can't help me."

"I wish I could." He shrugged his massive shoulders.

"Anyway give me a thought." I slid off the bar stool. We exchanged snappy waves and once again I was on the streets of Stratford, weary and hungry. I tried to jingle the coin in my pocket, but could produce only a faint rustling sound. I needed something to eat and I needed a place to sit down and think. I supposed that Father Wallop would feed and shelter me, and I felt fairly confident that I could force myself into Bartie Barstairs' home, but both of those retreats were interminable blocks away.

I had not been at my best during the day, a day of trudging drudgery, of posturing, of whining, of obsequious pleading. Not for many a year had *all* my artifices failed completely. What would a real addict do? Would he have the trouble that I had? I knew that one in the grip of true addiction simply couldn't have stood the gruelling series of humiliations that I had submitted myself to, all of them somehow summarized and capped by the inane exchange with the cretin bartender in his crepuscular bar. Would an addict go with unerring instinct to the hideout of the pusher? I counted what possibilities remained that I hadn't explored during the day. There was still the toilet in the movie house, and of course *Pardonnez Moi*. It seemed late enough to try that place and thither I directed my stumpy steps.

I found it, if not exactly as I left it, at least very much as I first found it. The unlighted sign still swung before the narrow door in the brick wall; within, the same naked and fly-specked light globes illumined the tomby room. What appeared to be the same duffel-coated couples sprawled in what appeared to be the same poses, poses expressive of world-weariness and of careful scrutiny of weekly photo journals that showed the latest fashions in *Weltschmerz*. The young ones who sprawled with such exquisite languor might have felt that they were *au courant*, but I felt on entering the joint for the second time that I was on some great and dreadful treadmill that kept me running, running, running as insipid scenes of Life in Stratford passed shakily by me.

I shuffled to a table in the far corner and slumped into an authentic pose. In time the waitress drew near. She expressed great boredom in my presence and an unreadiness to listen to my order. We exchanged blank looks half-filled with rue.

"You remember me?"

"Remember you!" she replied with a pretty half-sneer. I remembered her, of course.

"You remember me all right," I said.

"So? Like I got a bad memory."

"I remember you. I've spent the whole day composing three hundred lines of iambic trimeter. It's a description of you. It's part of the epic I'm composing on the life of King Farouk."

"Yeh, how's it go?"

"That part about you?"

"You're kidding about that."

"No, I'm not. Listen:

> Bifurcate manatee
> Who came from womby sea
> Not to Farouk's *Midi*
> But to *Pardon Me....*"

"*Pardonnez Moi,*" she said, compelled by pride, or passion for scholarly accuracy.

"I couldn't think of a rime for *moi.*"

"It's easy to rime. You just go through the alphabet putting each letter in front of the sound, like for *moi* you would say *ahwah, bwah, cwah....*" She continued silently for some moments. "The only word that's very good," she said finally, "is *whwah*. And that isn't very good."

"No."

"It's tough."

"I've been on Bennies all day," I said, "just trying for that one rime. Now I need something stronger."

"Like what?"

"Like anything stronger."

"Not here."

"Not now anyway, I see. I'm waiting for a guy."

"What guy?" We looked at each other coolly for a moment, then she dropped her gaze. She had made some kind of an admission with her question and I tried to dwell on her slip.

"Like, should I stand on my chair and shout his name?"

"You know him, huh?"

"He carries me on his book. Look, I'm broke, real broke. I can either sit here and wait for him or I can sit here and drink a beer while I wait for him. The decision is up to you."

"Well, I guess I can sneak you a beer this evening."

"You're a real girl. And listen, when he comes in, send him over here right away, like okay?"

"Yah, okay." She undulated off, returned in a few minutes with a bottle of locally brewed beer. It was swill but I drank. In a very few minutes I realized that I would never hear from the priest's charitable breakfast again. The memory was sweet but the breakfast was too far in the past to offer a noticeable retardation effect to the flat and fishy brew I foolishly gulped.

Sometime later my sylph brought another bottle; I noticed that the folk singers were with us again, nasally intoning ersatz work songs. There was no sign of the punk. I drank unthinkingly; again the waitress was at my side with more beer. "Like we have poetry and jazz readings here on Wednesdays," she said. "Will you come and read that stuff about me?"

"Yep," I said, groping for the fresh bottle.

Time, marked only by monotonous repetition of "John Henry he was a steel driving man," passed. Again the waitress returned. I glanced dizzily up and realized that it was not the waitress. I wish I could say that the stark realization that *he* stood before me made me instantly sober. As a matter of fact, I could *say* it, but the truth is I was not a whit more sober, and *he*, not the anticipated pusher, was only the long-time night student from the Friday evening class at Saint Felicitas: the bland pottage, the anonymous, whey-faced student whom I had distantly known in Chicago.

"I saw you sitting here alone, Professor Withers, and I wondered if you were all right."

"Wonder about that a bit myself. What are you doing here?" He settled in a chair across from mine.

"Well, there's not much to do in Stratford, you know." The waitress brought two more bottles of beer and a glass for my friend. He poured a jigger or so into his glass while I ignored the half-filled glass and drank a salty draught from the bottle itself. I had forgotten the glass and remembered it only because I knocked it off the table as I plopped the fresh beer bottle down.

"Whoops, well, let that pass. What are you doing here, uh, did I ever know your name?"

163

"Actually, it's Edward West; I believe I told you when we met in the supermarket."

"That's right, you did. You told me how to find this place too."

"A funny thing about that meeting; you know, while I was talking to you somebody stole my market cart, walked right off with it."

"Too bad. Have to pay for it?"

"Well, of course not. You see, it actually happened while I was talking to you. I left my cart by the front of the store and had just stepped back to get some paper napkins when I saw you."

"It was a roll of shelf paper."

"No. No." He spoke with what seemed undue emphasis. "I took only a packet of paper napkins."

"Say, that's pretty good. I'll bet I can't say that, not in my state. Listen: pick a packet of paper papkins. . . . I didn't do bad at all." I drank again from the bottle, wiped my beard with my sleeve, and squinted about the room. It was more smoke-filled, or at least it seemed more fuzzy to me. There were more people but the place wasn't crowded. West shifted to look about too.

"Are you waiting for someone?" he asked.

"No, no."

"Have I barged in on something?"

"No, no. Well, yes. Listen, West, I need a fix." At least I hadn't shocked him; he drummed delicately on the sides of his nearly full bottle of beer. His expression remained as bland as ever.

164

"I didn't know you were hooked, Professor Withers."

"Not hooked, West. It's just that I need one now."

"You weren't on narcotics in Chicago."

"Yes I was; well, no I wasn't. Not when I knew you. Anyway, the point is that I want one now. You know this place; can I get one here? The waitress seemed to imply . . . Well, have I made myself clear? I mean, I'm hoping that she'll send the pusher over here." It was difficult to tell how much all that beer churning about in my stomach was affecting my speech. I was willing to concede some garbling, but I thought that I had made my point clear nevertheless. I found it particularly difficult to talk to West because his pudding face gave neither encouragement nor indication of bewilderment. He minded pouring beer into his glass, but even then the bottom of the glass was barely covered.

"You won't get anything tonight, Professor."

"No? What do you know, West?"

"The heat's on. I have these artist friends that I told you about. It's why I come here actually. They tell me that the heat has been on since last Thursday. Everything's closed down."

"Yes, I feared that." I took another pull at my bottle, settled it carefully on the table and slumped down in my chair. I imagined envious looks, calculating glances of admiration turned on my slump. Tomorrow night *Pardonnez Moi* would exhibit dozens of imitation Witherslumps. I cast my arms on the table top, supported myself on my forearms and allowed only the back of my neck and the base of my spine to touch the chair. The pose was genuine. All day long I had been suppressing the dark suspicion that the news of Linda Brusick's death had driven the peddlers and pushers into darkest hiding. My tiring search had been foredoomed by the newspaper accounts of her suicide.

I looked unsteadily at Edward West sitting across from me. There was something there that didn't meet the eye. Perhaps it was the vague realization of his hidden depths that sent a faint trickle of new thought wending down the beery currents of my mind. Like the Gulf Stream, its edges not distinct but the main current clearly distinguishable, the suspicion formed through weariness, ennui, and growing biliousness. Why Thursday? If Linda Brusick's body had not been discovered until late Saturday night or early Sunday morning, why had the sale of narcotics stopped on Thursday?

"Hey, Eddie ole boy, what do you mean, the heat's on?"

"Well, you know. I mean, actually I get all my information from various friends."

"Do your friends mean to suggest that the police in Stratford connive with narcotic sellers?"

"I don't think they mean that. Let's face it, this is a pretty small town. The police probably know something about everything that goes on. I mean, if it goes on, there must be some, well, tacit knowledge on the part of the police."

"How long will the heat be on, do you think?"

"*I* don't know anything about it. My friends say until Wednesday or later, depending on the outcome of the coroner's hearing into Linda Brusick's death tomorrow."

I felt suddenly tired, worthless, drunken, unimportant. And short. "I got to go," I said, shuffling my feet in several haphazard directions. "Need sleep. Go night-night."

"Can I give you a ride, Professor?" My eyes suddenly filled with tears of gratitude; that someone should offer to drive me home . . . it was overwhelming. I sniffled.

"You're too good by far, West. Far West, that's good."

"Where are you staying?" He offered me a steadying hand.

"The college," I said remembering the luxury of Jim Downey's comfortable bed and his banjo seat pajamas. "The cottage at the cottage, the college's college . . . the college on the campus . . . the little cottage on the edge of the cottage."

We shuffled from *Pardonnez Moi* without much dignity. I remember something of the ride, of a walk along the lake. West seemed to have left me at the iron gates. Downey's cottage was still terribly befouled, but I negotiated the ruins of his life, made my goal — his rumpled bed — and slept.

Chapter 8

THE RINGING OF THE TELEPHONE awoke me. I do not believe that Alexander Graham Bell, that kindly man ("Mr. Watson, I want you"), invented the telephone *bell*. The ring is so strident, so commandingly shrill, so diabolically timed: BrrrrrrRING, pause, pause, pause. I do believe it has stoppedBRRRRRingNG. I feel that the bell in its present state could have only evolved. There must have been a series of monstrous mutations in the Bell Laboratories, bells that were sports but whose calls were so disgusting that they demanded immediate attention. The technicians, deprived no doubt by that time of the gentle guidance of Alex, in panic and dismay turned their attention to these terrible mutations. The proto-bells, whose melodious sound was a muted tinkly version of that happy lilting call, "Mr. WwwwwAHTsonsonson," fell into decay because of lack of attention.

No sound on earth can so wake a sleeper as that of the telephone. I awoke, each nerve jangling inharmoniously, my muscles tensed to leap toward the vile instrument. I fought that impulse. I am one of those rare men who can sit in a room alone with a ringing telephone and refuse to answer it. I am proud to be able to make that statement and I write it with some pride. I can sit alone in a room with a ringing telephone and refuse to answer it.

I did it once. Of course, I was almost out of my mind by the time that the ringing stopped. It rang seven and one-half times. And my mental condition grew steadily worse throughout the rest of that long ago afternoon. That happened in a room that I lived in one summer session at Chicago. By early evening it was clear that I would have to find out who had tried to call me before I could address myself to my textbooks. I started by casually calling a friend to see if he had tried to get in touch with me. He protested innocence of the call and so I tried another. And then another.

I made nearly a hundred calls; the last dozen or so were long distance calls. At midnight I found myself calling an old army buddy whom I hadn't thought of for over three years. My call revealed that *he* hadn't thought of me for nearly five years. I have never discovered who was trying to call me that afternoon. I had to move to another room, and that one quite a ways from the campus too, before the landlady caught a glimpse of her telephone bill. But I can sit in a room alone with a ringing telephone and refuse to answer it.

I did it once. In Jim Downey's cottage, however, impulse won out over will. Despite the warmth of the bed, and despite the certain knowledge that I would have to turn on the bright overhead light and search through the room for the cursed instrument, despite deep assurance that the call was neither for me nor important, I crept out of bed and fumbled for the light switch.

It was still dark, but I felt a good deal better than I had felt upon retiring. I groped among the books and papers strewn about the front room until I discovered the receiver.

"Hallo?"

"Stuff for sale." The voice was unfamiliar.

"What?"

"The heat's off. Stuff for sale."

"Do you know who you're talking to?"

Silence on the wire.

"This isn't Jim Downey," I said. Still silence. "This is Red Withers."

"Do you want to make business?"

"Yah, sure. Keeno."

"*Pardonnez Moi, toute de suite.*" The French accent was even stranger than the normal voice.

"Well, isn't it late?"

"Not that late." The dead sound told me that my caller had hung up. I depressed the button, then dialed Operator.

"Operator." It was a depressingly nasal voice.

"Can you tell me what time it is, honey?"

"Dial Main one two one two for the time signal."

"I tried that but there seems to be something wrong."

"Oh?"

"Do you happen to know the time?"

"Well . . . it's about twelve-thirty." I hung up. Had it been a coin phone I would have had the correct time and my dime

170

back. As it was, Jim Downey was saved the expense of one call. For me, it was back to the treadmill.

In the bedroom I found that my shoes, my socks and the cuffs of my trousers were water soaked. My stumbling circumference of the lake must have been drawn with a narrower radius than safety, or at least comfort, dictated. Could I have been — on what in memory seemed a fuzzy but fully realized scene of walking along the edge of the lake on my way to the cottage — could I have been wading drunkenly in the marge? My soaked socks seemed prim evidence. But if it were so, why didn't I feel worse than I did? Or did I?

I shook my head vigorously; all seemed well above. There were no dull pains, no stabbing attacks, no waves of nausea. I felt fine. And my quest was drawing to a close. Could I, like the little tailor who killed seven flies with one blow, with one blow discover the villain responsible for Linda's death, settle my score with nasty Chief of Detectives Salter, and confirm my employment at Saint Felicitas? And what if I were to discover Jim Downey too? There was sudden return of an abandoned thought: could he be behind it all?

The first question to settle was the one of rapid (toot sweet) transportation to *Pardonnez Moi*. Should I walk? Take a bus? Ride Bartie Barstairs piggyback? Dare I take a taxi?

I tried to calculate my chances: would there be on duty at this time of a Tuesday morning either a taxi driver who had worked on Thursday afternoon or one who had worked late on Sunday morning? Taxi service was indisputably fast and reliable, and I felt that there was enough at stake to risk it again. I called the taxi company and ordered a cab to meet me at the college gates in ten minutes.

Back in the bedroom I contemplated the soaked cuffs of my trousers. The evidence of a thoughtless stroll through the marshy lake was too overwhelming to deny any longer. From the heap that Brusick and his mobsters had left on the floor, I found two dry socks, not a pair, and slipped them on before wedging my feet into my wet shoes and pulling on my damp trousers. Hastily I pulled forth one of Downey's suitcases, filled it with the clothes and books nearest at hand and snapped it shut. In the course of my awkward trot to the college gates I had cause to curse my integrity. I had carried realism a bit too far; the heavy suitcase banged against my ankle bone.

The taxi was waiting; I did not give myself time to hesitate. I threw open the front door and tossed in the heavy suitcase. If I had to run, I didn't want to be encumbered with that weighty thing.

"You the guy that ordered the cab?" he asked. The voice was new to me, but that man was my friend. I could have embraced him. But I didn't. I crept quickly into the back of the cab lest he see my beard and be reminded of what might be current stories of deadbeats among his own kind.

"Das wight," I said in my Eric von Stroheim voice. "Yah, ich order ein cob."

"Where to, Doc?" He flicked down the metal flag; the meter immediately registered thirty-five cents and jumped to fifty before he had shifted gears. I felt justified.

"Dake me to dee ayreporrt, danke. But virst vee must shtopb at the *Polizei*, dah boleece station, yah?"

172

"The police station, huh?" His cab glided swiftly away from the campus.

"Yah. Id's embarrazing. In my how you say leedle boyhood ich bin ein Nazi. Very bad. Now ich must register with *Polizei* wheneber ich go ein place to anudder vrom."

"Kinda rare for a guy like you to be in Stratford. You been speaking at the college, huh?"

"Yah."

We lapsed into silence, he apparently rehearsing our dialogue, practicing my dialect so that he could tell his wife about his adventure when he met her in the morning. He would have more than this to tell her.

Down the darkened streets of Stratford we whisked, the taxi meter clicking regularly, seventy-five, eighty-five, ninety-five. The business district was deserted. The pale globes of the police station shone blocks ahead. The taxi pulled quietly to the curb and I stepped briskly out.

"Keeb the meter wunning, yah?"

"Don't you worry, buddy boy."

I was playing the game for high stakes. The ante was my own cherished body, for that matter. But if the law of averages meant anything at all, if it were a meaningful construct, I would not meet lumbering Dan, the creeping policeman, as I hurried up the steps for the third time in as many nights. I pushed open the front door, shot down the dusty corridor, flung open the side door through which Dan had once so roughly propelled me, and plunged into the dark alleyway. I had made it!

I counted on the heavy suitcase that the taxi driver held in protective custody. With that weighty bag by his side he would not grow restive or suspicious for some time. My object was to cross the street and beat a way to *Pardonnez Moi,* riverward of the station some seven blocks, before the cabbie awoke to the hoax. I circled the police building at a run, spurted across the street and pressed myself flat against a darkened store front on the opposite side. From there I could see the cabbie sitting patiently at the wheel of his extortion machine, his wrists folded across the steering wheel. He seemed confident that he was the only one playing the game of graft in Stratford that night. It was outrageous that he should try to charge a dollar and a quarter for the short ride from the campus. With controlled indignation I turned and limped hastily away, toward *Pardonnez Moi.* My wet shoes gave pain but I was a crusader.

For the third time I pushed open the filthy door of the designated rendezvous. The room was empty, silent, unreal, even darker than before. One dusty light globe high in the blackened rafters only emphasized the darkness.

Pardonnez Moi was obviously closed for the night, the unlocked door unlocked for my convenience. I walked to the center of the room, my gait the unseemly result of impatience and caution. There was still no evidence of occupancy — the chairs empty, the arena bare, the bar to the rear dark and drear. Again I advanced, but now more deeply into shadow with the single light globe to my back.

There was a sudden whirr, a blast of colored lights that struck my eyes painfully: red, mauve, blue, yellow, green lights whirled across the roof and rafters. There was a sharp metallic sound (the hammer of a gun?) and then the electronic melody of a terribly magnified violin hit me. Someone

174

had plugged in the juke box. "The Little Gypsy Tea Room" hit me, encompassed me with the brisk ululations of Guy Lombardo's regimented musicians. The recording was poor but I was worse. I sank shakily into the nearest chair.

"Why, Professor Withers, are you back so soon?" The unction of Edward West's voice was plain. I looked over my shoulder to find him standing some paces behind my chair. His face was bland, unsmiling, as veiled as ever. I noted that his hands were carried in the pocket of his jacket.

"West, did you call me?" I asked.

"I took you home, remember?"

"Vaguely, yes. But did you call me?"

He strolled slowly to my table, snaked out with his foot the chair opposite mine and sat down.

"Call you?" he asked in what I was confident was mockery. I wished with a fervent wish that he would take his hands out of his pockets. Did he carry a gun, a knife, a needle, or a handful of dimes for the juke box? "Stick out your hands," he said, as though he had the same thought. I held out both hands, fingers extended, palms down. They trembled, there was no doubt of that. They trembled. I have since come to convince myself that my hands trembled from hunger. At the time, with chagrin, I acknowledged fear. He attributed the shake to another cause.

"You're hooked all right."

"Like heck I'm hooked."

"Like anything. You can put your hands down now." He smiled that mediocre smile of his. "I had my doubts about your story this evening. I mean, the way you swilled the beer, I thought you were a man who got his kicks from three-point-two beer. But then I figured, I could tell for sure by how fast you got down here after my call. I mean, let's face it, you're actually not a fellow much given to altruism. If you made it down here in less than fifteen minutes, it must be because you needed a fix. And needed it bad. Let me see your arm."

"No."

"Well, that confirms it, I guess. The heat's off for a while. Incidentally, did you get the significance of 'My Little Gypsy Tea Room?' I mean, if you're on tea." His smile, which he turned on me, was, once you saw the veil, one of purest evil. I suddenly thought how pleasant it would be just then to be safely asleep in that perfectly delightful day cot of Father Wallop's. Dim patterns formed behind the pressing wish to be safely away.

"You're the dope pusher," I said, thinking aloud. He inclined his head satirically.

"You should get an 'A' for the course, *Professor*."

"And that's why you take classes at colleges — Chicago, here, places you go."

"Your acumen, considering you are a *professor*, fills me with astonishment." I was frightened for one thing, and ideas were pushing belligerently forward in my mind to receive acknowledgment and ticketing — and with all that, a sudden sickening sense of guilt and connivance welled up. I was appalled at my own lack of sophistication. Slowly I let the guilty phrases trickle out in words.

"And you hang around the college campuses hoping that

176

the teachers will put enough pressure on the students to turn them desperate enough to try your palliatives."

"Well, you've done your bit to help me too — as a student, I mean. The student who does the assignment just a little bit better than the rest of the class always makes my business a bit more brisk. It was good to have you in one of my classes, *Professor*."

"I think you're a sod."

"You're hooked all right; the reaction is right. Let me tell you that I have nothing but contempt for you and for all addicts. Hopheads, mainliners, smokers, you're all weak and contemptible. Listen, I've been handling dope for seven years now; do you think that I haven't had problems during that time? But I didn't try to run from them. I didn't bury my head in a snow pile; I didn't sink into self-pity. I hate you all and I ought to make you dance for this." With a flourish he pulled his right hand from the pocket of his jacket and dropped a small fold of white paper on the table. "I ought to make you dance and sing too. You want it, don't you?" With the same flourish he scooped up the little envelope.

"Wait a minute," I cried as a new pattern suddenly formed. "Sing? Singer. You pass yourself off as a sewing machine salesman, don't you. Singer Sewing. The Canary. Are you the Canary?"

"That's right, teacher. And the next time you need some powder you just ask for the Canary." He flipped the white paper envelope across the table to me.

"You know I can't pay," I said. "I told you I was broke. I really am."

177

"*This* time it's on the house. I've had great success with collaborators before. You're one down to me now and don't you forget it. Now get out of here. I'll be around when the shakes come back to you. And they will," he said as I stood up. "They will. They will."

I scooped up the white envelope; it was the evidence I had been seeking.

"And you're the one who hooked Linda Brusick?"

"*You* ought to know better. The truth is that all you meatheads hook yourselves. I sold her the stuff, sure. I met her in your evening class, sure. That's why I'm enrolled in the class. It stinks, incidentally. Maybe next time I'll have you recite the Mumbo bit backwards before I do business." My professional pride was stung, and under that humiliation another pattern took shape. I remembered the scene at the supermarket and the market cart that I had purloined. What had I paid for? Tea, and powdered sugar, and. . . .

"Just how much do you cut your dope with powdered sugar?" I said.

"I don't cut it at all, Professor."

"Then why do you buy all that powdered sugar? And tea, and yes, not paper napkins, but a roll of shelf paper to wrap this stuff in?"

"Are you the sod that stole my cart?"

I would have answered, but my feet were suddenly in control and I was in full flight. Edward West's mocking voice followed me to the door.

"When you pass the juke box, will you push number twenty-two? 'I Get Along Without You Very Well.'"

178

I let the door of *Pardonnez Moi* close behind me for the last time. On the sidewalk I stopped and breathed deeply of the sharp and nipping autumn air. It would snow soon. Snow? I glanced at the folded bit of paper in my hand, then shoved it into the pocket of my jacket. I needed time to think, but at the same time I felt a compulsion to move. And where should I go?

At first blush it would seem that my duty was to report my knowledge of dope traffic to the police, but several reasons prompted caution. The more I thought, the more reasons I uncovered why I should stay away from the police. There was, for one, what could at the most charitable interpretation be described as violent and personal antipathy of Chief of Detectives George Salter for my humble self. His damaged car would have only fed his irrational and groundless hatred. Again, there would probably still be an unpaid taxi parked in front of the police station. Lastly, there was the caution induced by the dim feeling that official Stratford knew pretty well what the Stratford underworld was up to.

If a report to the police seemed a chancy thing, what was left? I could tell Bartie Barstairs and thus mark his unborn child but accomplish little else. Of course, my contract *was* with the priest. If I awoke him in the middle of the night he might be disgruntled, but I could already imagine the disgruntled look fading from his sleep-filled face as joy for his parish, delight in a plan well executed, and sheer admiration for me struggled to be primarily expressed in his rugged and broken countenance. I would tell Father Wallop.

Head down, feet clogging along in a weary but determined

dogtrot, I started for the heart of the city. At some time in my journey I would be forced to cross Western Avenue, but I planned to run parallel to that street until well out of range of the parked and patient taxi.

An oblique glance at a passing car stirred an uneasy memory. It was, I realized with a rush, in this very block that someone had shot at me the evening before. The spot had been well chosen by the bungling assassin. But for that dear and lovely tree there was no escape, no shelter for a block in either direction. Ahead of me I saw the headlights of a slow-moving car. The lights swept the walls of the warehouse opposite as the car turned and started down my street. Instantly I slowed to a walk and turned my head toward the wall on my side of the street, away from the approaching car. It crept slowly by me. I did not look at it, but the quiet sound assured me that this car was not the mangled remnant of George Salter's prized machine.

The car passed me. I heard the impressive roar of the too-powerful engine as it suddenly sped up and whooshed away. I chanced a glance over my shoulder and saw the car swerve sharply around at the intersection to bear back in my direction. In panic I burst into a run. There was no direction to go but ahead; on either side of the street spread blank brick walls. Ahead the block stretched to infinity. I broke my run and cut back, heading for the shelter of that cherished tree, but I knew as I turned that it was too late. The car was upon me, swinging across the street.

How does one fend off a bullet? My hands flew to my eyes, my ears, my crotch, my stomach. I crouched forward, twisting awkwardly to the ground. I have never been strong on dignity, and I chose to meet death with great, quivering reluctance. The auto halted at the curb, its headlights upon me; four doors whacked open and hundreds of large, black-suited men poured out. Among their number — the number dwindled to four as I recognized them — were Thumbs Brusick, Gnome Tabor, and two thugs of a more common stamp.

Crouching forward on my bruised knees and trembling hands, I looked unsteadily up. Tabor spoke first.

"It's the geek from the school."

"Hey, thanks for the light," I said. "I seem to have dropped some money, nearly fifty bucks." I felt forward with my right hand, sweeping the sidewalk. Tabor kicked viciously at my hand and Thumbs grunted a warning.

"Stand up, slob." I stood. We looked uneasily at each other for a while, then Thumbs spoke to his thugs. He inclined his head in their direction, spoke from the corner of his mouth, but tried to fix me with his eyes. "You think he's the guy?"

"Every pill roller in town said he had been in trying to buy dope," Tabor said. "Look, Thumbs, let the guys hold him up against the wall and I'll get the car and smash him with it." He gestured in a perfectly sickening fashion, his right fist driving into his yielding and crumpling left palm. "Like kapow!"

"You the slob who hooked my Linda?" Thumbs exhibited a visible effort at control.

"I don't even know her. I was terribly sorry to hear about her death. . . . But I'm not a dope pusher. I know who is, though."

"Yeh, you know him real well. Real personal." It was Tabor, still grinding his grimy fist into his filthy left paw.

"But you *can't* think that I sold dope to Linda. I was never in this town before. Not until Thursday."

"You say."

"But it's true."

"Search him," Thumbs snapped. "Turn around, you, and throw your hands against the wall."

"I will *not*," I said, turning around and throwing my palms flat against the brick wall. I had seen the menacing forward step of his three crude mechanicals.

The search was in large part a series of rough and obscene slaps directed to the seams of my outraged body. Tabor thumped the right pocket of my jacket and I said, "There's nothing there. There's nothing in there." He plunged his toady hand into the pocket and produced the paper packet.

"You bastid," Thumbs said. "I swore I'd kill the man who sold the stuff to Linda. And I will."

"Now, *loook, I didn't*. . . ." The gnome drove a horned elbow into my kidney. It was a terrible blow and a great hurt that I quite promptly forgot under the following circumstances. Three days later I had occasion to examine the purplish splotch and wonder for a moment or two where I had acquired the injury.

Tabor was carried away with his own enthusiasm. "Thumbs, buddy, you stand right here; and the boys will spread-eagle the geek against the wall. Then I'll get into the car and hit him. So you can see it all, see? I'll hit him easy

182

the first time and then crack him twice more when he starts down."

"HALP," someone cried. I was the only one of the quintet who needed help, so I assume that I was the one who called, "HALP! HALP!" But I was as startled as they. We all look suspiciously around, I for the person who had cried out with such volume, they to see if anyone had heard the cry. Their instinctive search showed that they knew less about the neighborhood than I did. There were no homes within three or four blocks; there was no one to hear my calls and it was foolish to cry out, as I did once again, "HALP, HALP, HALP."

Help turned the corner only a block away and drove down the narrow street. It was a black-and-white police car and I resolved on the spot never again to entertain theological doubts. The red searchlight atop the police car flicked suddenly on and added to the glare of the headlights in which we stood: a tableau which left no doubt as to which was the oppressed, who were the oppressors. The police car stopped; everything paused for a moment, then cautiously from the driver's side emerged Dan the Hairy Policeman, a riot rifle held in his meaty hands with professional competence.

I sobbed. A sob is the only true expression of ambiguous emotion. Salter, dressed in a dark suit, no weapon visible, emerged from the police car. He and Thumbs examined each other with professional curiosity.

"Brusick?"

"You Salter?"

"Me Tarzan," I said, rushing forward to stand between

them. I saw that no good could come from a liaison between my arch-enemies. "These four gentlemen were going to chop me up with that car right there." I pointed out the offending exhibit. "Right there. See it? I think you should impound the car, arrest them, and let me go."

"What's up, Brusick?" Salter asked.

"A little private business."

"My eye! They were going to *kill* me. Look, they think I sold dope to Linda. Of course, I didn't. But listen, I know who did. I spent the whole day walking around this stupid town [shouldn't have said that] and I finally found out who's peddling dope to everybody, and these stupid guys [shouldn't have said that, either] think that *I'm* the one that sells the stuff. But listen, I'm not. That ought to convince you." I had the feeling that no one was listening to me. Brusick and Salter were engaged in a private contest, apparently trying to determine which of them would drop his gaze first. The three thugs affected total indifference.

"I can tell you who sells dope. I just now found out. I know who sold it to Linda!"

Salter flicked his head toward Dan, who abruptly turned back to climb into the police car.

"I thought that this was a holdup or something," Salter said, and he and Brusick beamed and looked away. "You fellahs just go ahead and have your fun. Just don't, you know, disturb the police."

"You mean, like disturb the peace?" said Gnome Tabor.

"No," said Salter.

But I was running again, running down the street with the

speed of absolute desperation, zigzagging every so often as I remembered having seen Victor McLaglen zigzag in the movies of my youth. But running pell-mell. I left them all in the pool of automotive lights, nodding their heads in mutual satisfaction. I felt that I was still gaining speed when I fell. It was a terrible tumble and my first reaction was one of anger. I thought that Tabor had dealt me another knock; but even as I slithered on the rough sidewalk I knew that Tabor and his companions were at least half a block away. I scrambled to my feet running, staggered, zagged, zigged, accomplished the corner, turned but kept my pace. Another block I ran. The first sight of the residential area added speed to my legs.

I shot madly across the first lawn, hurdled a low picket fence, dashed through a barren backyard, vaulted a second fence and ran stumbling down a pitch-dark alley. Yet another block I ran until my lungs were dry and empty, until my legs flailed wildly beneath, until — praise heavens — I spotted a narrow angle between a garage and a backyard incinerator. The area was dark and too small for a human, but I squeezed easily into it. I crouched facing the alley and gasped for air.

Only then was I aware of the pain like fire in my shoulder. My exploring left hand encountered a warm and sticky mat. I was shot. I had been shot. I, Red Withers, had been shot at and hit. I hate blood. It has always struck me as a beastly substance. It is repellent to the touch, noxious to look at, revolting to taste, and nearly impossible to wash out of hankies. I do not like to imagine that thick and bloody juice moving around within me and I am shocked to imagine it just standing stagnant, as it someday will.

I could not bring myself to explore the wound in my shoulder; hastily I withdrew my sticky hand and wiped it vigorously on my jacket. I held my breath for a moment and turned my ears to the sounds of pursuit. I heard only the pounding of my heart as it — I was then confident — emptied the contents of my veins and arteries through the bullet wound onto the cold stones of the alleyway. I tried to analyze my feelings, to assay the pain in an attempt to determine the seriousness of the wound. Was it what the newspapers called in cavalier fashion a mere flesh wound, or had some vital organ been damaged? I tried to move my right arm, but the cramped quarters of my chosen oubliette prevented movement. Would I finally be removed by an impassive garbage man? Would I be fed to swine?

I struggled to rise but the pain struck. The pain that I should have felt when the bullet hit my shoulder and drove me to the sidewalk as I fled the unholy alliance of Salter and Brusick, that pain finally caught up with me. The incinerator seemed to fall away from me, the ground on which I hunkered undulated and I fainted.

When I awoke I was stiff and nauseated. I do not know how long I was unconscious. The back of my shirt was cold and clammy, the edge of my collar stiff with dried blood. I had not died, peace to Brusick or Tabor or whoever had shot me. A throaty groan, somehow reassuring, rolled from me as I struggled to my feet and staggered slowly down the alley. I tried to recall all of the scenes of Stratford that I had visited during the day. Had I passed any signs that proclaimed the home of a doctor? Feebly I cursed the foolish attitude of the medical profession that frowned upon doctors' placing flashing neon signs above their homes. An alert young doctor seeking a practice might do worse than to prowl the midnight alleys of Stratford. Had I noticed a black-and-gilt sign as I left the rectory of Father Wallop that morning? I could not be sure but I stumbled in that direction. If there were no doctors on the route I would simply present myself to the priest and request the Last Sacraments. I would die sweetly at his guilty feet, guilty because he had got me into the search in the first place. Perhaps I would withhold my dying forgiveness and that would prey on his mind for a long time.

Once in the course of my erratic walk I saw a moving automobile and then I hid behind a withering hedge. Twice I crumpled to the curb and retched dryly. I was alternately hot and cold, chilled and feverish, numb and crippled with pain, when finally I turned down the street of Father Wallop's church. There, directly across from the rectory, I found the sign that I had dimly remembered. It was black and gilt, its lettering discreet enough to attest to the high ethics of its sponsor: J. J. Johnston, M.D. The sign placed in the middle of the front lawn of an old but imposing house was wired for lights but no electric bulb shone in the bracket above the black border. Either J. J. Johnston couldn't afford such an expense or he was too rich to need advertisement even so unobtrusive as this. I was clear, however, that at one time he had welcomed after-dark business. I pushed the brass doorbell without hesitation.

Eventually there was noise within the house; a thump or two and then lights flashed on, blocking out squares of light on the sere grass of the front lawn. A bolt shot back, the front door swung inward and I saw the doctor. He was a big man, young, large, fat and balding. Sparse yellow hair sprayed out from his smooth head, forming a nimbus in the light of his hallway. During business hours he must have plastered the hair across the top of his freckled skull. He was wrapped in a black-and-silver robe of tentlike proportions. A glance at my bloodstained coat and at my Rejected Martyr stance prompted a motherly cluck from his cherubic mouth.

"Listen," I said. "Do you have two aspirins?"

"Come on," he said gently, and as gently he grasped my arm and led me through the hall and into his office. The room was a combination study and office; there were shelves of books, a large desk, a glass-front cabinet of shiny tools and a leather-topped table upon which he settled me. "All right now. There you are. Now, what happened?"

"Well, I have this headache."

"I'll bet you do." He turned toward the cabinet. "Can you take morphine?" he asked, rummaging briskly through a metal drawer.

It was, I suppose, ironical. If I had only possessed the sense to have myself shot early that morning I could have found a drug dispenser without leaving Father Wallop's block.

"I never turn down a free drink, Doc."

He squinted at the hypodermic needle as he turned and squinted at me as he spoke. "This isn't exactly a drink. And this isn't exactly a free clinic. I hope you don't think *that*."

"Go ahead and shoot. If you want to save time you can give me morphine and perforate my Blue Cross Card with one jab." The squint left his bland young face when I said the words of the incantation: Blue Cross. The guilt that I might have felt at telling a lie was outweighed by the satisfaction I received in calming and assuring the young fellow. Together we shucked off my coat, rolled my left sleeve and charged me with sweet oblivion. As from a great distance I watched him busy himself with my shoulder. His actions seemed ambiguous and unimportant. In time I grew bored with watching and stretched out on the table. The medicine man clucked at me in a knowing fashion and helped me to settle back. In time, undisturbed by his probing and plucking and fussing, I dreamed. It seemed as if he was rummaging in my wallet for that Blue Cross card; it turned out that this part was no dream. The rest of it was, though. I was pursued through streets narrow and endless. I was crushed by onrushing black automobiles. Hairy Dan the Policeman threw water in my face and George Salter poked his finger in my stomach.

I awoke to the sound of muffled speech in the next room. It was broad daylight and I was still on the leather-topped table, a blanket tucked solicitously under my beard. I sat upright, and muscle and bone protested. There was a commotion of notable volume in and between my vitals. Muscles called to me in pity; bones sang in anguish. My shoulder suddenly kindled and went up in flames. My mouth was in an unspeakable condition; I doubted that *any* therapy would suffice to restore *that* hutch to its once antiseptic condition.

On the floor beneath my table lay my clothes, fouled with blood and grime, apparently all of them slashed with Doctor

Johnston's finest surgical steel. My wallet, its worthless heap of non-identification cards spread before it, lay on the doctor's desk. I groaned aloud but only a dry click emerged. The voices, their meaning indistinguishable, continued on the other side of the door. I slid from the table to my shaky legs and fumbled my way into my doubled-heeled shoes. At least they were intact. The effort it took to drape the blanket about my shoulders was a noble one and I shall always think of myself fondly for having accomplished it. Thus wrapped, I stumbled to the door. The voices ceased as I tugged it open.

There was no one in the hallway. I staggered toward the front door.

"Yes?" said Doctor Johnston from behind me.

"I just thought I'd run down and report myself to the coroner."

"And he'd probably believe you for all he knows about medicine, but I'll make that report, Mr. Withers, if it becomes necessary. Just as I'll make the report about your gunshot wound."

"Gunshot wound!"

"Of course, you were shot."

"No wonder I didn't get the license number. I *thought* it was an awfully small truck."

He stood smiling at the door of his office. "If you'll just step back in here, I can look at that shoulder of yours and we can make arrangements for payment."

"Well, I don't know," I said, still clinging to the knob of the front door. "I don't want to take any more of your valuable time."

190

"You can't leave dressed like that, anyway. Come in here."

I followed him back into the office. There he showed me the bullet. It was dark, small, extremely ugly and the sight of it made me feel quite faint.

"It went right through you," he said with admiration. "But the force was spent by then and I found it lodged in the front lapel of your jacket. Frankly I've never treated a gunshot wound before. I found it quite interesting. Now in the back, the wound is simply of the puncture type, easy enough to treat. But in front, where the bullet emerged, things were torn quite a bit. You'll have a scar of course. Two of them, to be accurate."

I subsided against the table, heady with the sweet-sour taste of self-pity.

"I'm required to report all gunshot wounds. I've been comparing this bullet with some pictures I have in my Medico-Legal Dictionary. This bullet seems to have come from what they call a service revolver. Would you care to tell me what happened before I call the police?"

"I'd like to, Doc, but I wasn't even there when the shot was fired."

"Yes, well, shall we talk about arranging for the fee then? You seem to have neither money nor an affiliation with the Blue Cross."

"I'm sorry, Doc, I'm not at liberty to reveal my true identity."

"Have I stumbled across something *big?*"

"I can't even divulge that. I can only assure you that you will receive what you deserve in way of a fee." I sampled the pain in my shoulder again and at the pain I felt I knew how little he deserved in way of recompense.

A look of faint worry crossed his face, moving from east to west; when it had passed he seemed reconciled to not receiving an immediate payment for his Hippocratic ministrations. "I will have to report the gunshot wound to the police, you understand?"

"Naturally. Do you know the number?"

"Well, yes."

"Good. Tell them exactly what happened. I'm pretty sure they'll understand. Tell them that late last night, or rather early this morning, I came here wounded. I came from Father Wallop's house across the street. You repaired me. This morning I wrapped a blanket about my shoulders and returned to Father Wallop's."

"Oh, really."

"Watch." I pulled myself erect, clutched the blanket to my narrow chest and trundled to the door.

"You can't go out dressed that way," he said, but he opened the front door hesitantly.

"Just across the street." I was making good forward progress despite the lurches and lunges sideways, so I didn't dare to turn and wave.

He didn't close the door until I had rung the bell of the rectory. I could easily picture him, I could almost hear him clattering back to his telephone.

The priest himself opened the door to my ring. He was dressed in a neatly pressed black suit; a Roman collar of brilliant white celluloid encircled his short and swarthy neck. His black eyes narrowed as he took in my skimpy costume. He greeted me rather obliquely.

"On this very doorstep I have found newborn babies, flaming crosses, stolen bicycles, drunks, and once, a group of carollers from the Reformed Baptist Church, but how shall I describe you?"

"Just say: 'the Withered Rose.' "

"I rarely rise to such heights of rhetoric in my report to the Chancery."

"I seek asylum. Will you let me in?"

He stepped back and swung open the door. "What in the world happened to you?"

"I hope it wasn't a taste of things to come." The blanket slipped from my shoulder and he saw the inept bandage that Doctor Johnston had twisted about my poor shoulder.

"Oh, I say, I'm sorry. Do you drink beer with that arm?"

I thought it best to ignore his repartee until I felt more myself. I simply pushed beyond him and on to the sun porch where I settled in his own black wicker chair.

"That telephone," I said accusingly, "will ring in about one minute. Before it does: what do you think of the moon-faced malpractitioner across the way?"

"Johnston? I think little about him. He is given to dressing in nautical clothes, faded blue denims and all that, and to mowing his lawn during my sermon at the Sunday Mass. He has a high-powered gasoline engine on his lawn mower, but that's about all I know."

"While you were bandying words at the front door he was

making some pretty serious charges against you to the police."

"Oh?" Father Wallop said as the telephone rang.

I waited until his hand had encircled the telephone receiver before I spoke. "I know who peddles dope in your Stratford."

The priest's dark eyebrows quizzed me but he spoke into the phone. "Saint Perpetua's Rectory, Father Wallop speaking. . . . Oh, is that you, George? Just a moment, hang on will you?" He cupped the phone against his chest and addressed me. "Who?"

"You're talking to him."

"You?"

"No."

"I don't believe it."

"Then tell him. The two of you can have a good laugh." I twitched myself in the chair and pretended indifference. The gesture was not a success, nor was it pain that prevented me from carrying it out. I was suddenly carried back to the terrible days of my adolescence when I studied under the stern and untender guidance of soutaned Jesuits. My quondam mentors had made it a point of honor to call no boy for Latin recitation if there were the least hint that he had prepared his lesson. No smug-looking boy was ever called upon to parse or conjugate, for such an act would have led the boy into the sin of pride. The guilt-ridden, slack-jawed, pimply chinned boys were called to their feet one after the other, given a Latin verb to conjugate and, when the halting admission of incompetence or, more rarely, a thoroughly inept

194

attempt at bravado was produced, the thunder would strike. Desks would shudder, erasers would fly about our heads, fists would be raised in anger and supplication, tears would quiver in eyes long unused to flow. The trick was to look indifferent. If you knew the lesson and wished to exhibit your knowledge, the only hope was to look indifferent. Jesuits sometimes confounded that indifferent look with the smirk of the day-dreamer and would call upon you. On the other hand, if you had failed to con the assigned text the only hope of escape was to look indifferent. It was a faint hope, so often dashed. But sometimes a young Scholastic would mistake the look of indifference for the mock-indifference of the prepared scholar and so would pass you by. I had always been a shocking failure in my attempts at indifference.

And in that rectory, even though bearing under the tight and septic bandages of Johnston the red badge of courage and manhood, I nevertheless found myself unable to carry off my chosen pose. Under the rank and reddish growth of a Withering beard I felt again the conspicuous red blotches of the adolescent chin.

I looked, in a word, guilty as sin.

Father Wallop diverted his attention to the telephone. "Here again, George. I was just leaving the house for the Brusick inquest. Thought you'd be there by now. . . . Who? . . . Oh? And he's a parishioner of mine? Well, if you'll wait a mo. until I get the parish books. . . . Oh, he's *not* a member of the parish?"

There was a longish pause and then Father Wallop continued. "Well, George, have you checked Johnston's affiliations? I mean, don't most young doctors join the Youknow-whats? Maybe this is an initiation stunt? . . . Well, I don't really think it myself, but then how can we account for such a wild story? . . . Look, I'll see you at the inquest, how'll that be? . . . Good." He replaced the receiver and looked coldly at me.

"Have you proof?"

I struck my heart a painful blow as a reply.

"If you're right it will have to be a citizen's arrest. Do you understand what that is?"

"No, Father."

"Well, never mind for now. In any event you'll have to have other clothes. Other than a stolen and incriminating blanket."

"I have some stuff at Bartie Barstairs' home."

"I know the house. Well, the title 'servant of the servants' is one I don't disdain even if I don't covet it. You straggle along and take a sitz bath or shave or whatever you do. I'll drop over to Barstairs and retrieve some decent clothing. The coroner's inquest into Linda Brusick's death is at eleven this morning. It would be interesting if we could get you into the inquiry room for that."

Chapter 9

I STOOD BEFORE FATHER WALLOP: we had just emerged from his automobile which he had parked in a No Parking Zone in front of the Stratford Municipal Building. The building was one block trainward of the police building. I stood as best I was able, shaved, sitzed, dressed in my original shoes and an odd suit of Bartie's. Perhaps I sagged a bit but the sag was unnoticeable within the folds of that suit.

"I don't know how we are going to get you into the inquiry," he said. "Tell me again. Are you *sure* that George Salter is the dope peddler?"

"No, he doesn't sell it. A guy named Edward West — or at least a guy who calls himself that — sells the stuff. Incidentally, there he goes into the Municipal Building. The ghoul. Do you think he is coming to the inquest?"

"If what you say is true, he might be simply renewing his dope-peddler license. You have no proof?"

"Only the heat. And the fact that everyone seems to know that dope has a demi-official okay."

197

"The heat?"

"You know, what goes on and off. It's recognized permission to engage in illegal trade. Football lotteries, bingo games [he winced], dope — when the heat's off they flourish. Well, the heat had nothing to do with Linda Brusick's death. Things closed down the day Jim Downey disappeared, not the day that Linda dropped from sight. And the heat went off last night, the night before the inquest. Which means that the heat, and I think that means Chief of Detectives Salter, has nothing to fear from the inquest. And it means too, now that I think of it, that he has no more worries about Jim Downey, whose disappearance apparently forced him to clamp down."

"You think Jim's dead?"

I shrugged. My shoulder cautioned me against repeating that gesture.

"Do you think we can prove anything at the inquest?"

I shrugged again and received a more imperative reminder from my shoulder.

"Do you want to chance it?"

I refused to shrug. I was equally adamant about nodding my head. I surely didn't *want* to be in the same room with Edward West and Thumbs Brusick and George Salter.

Father Wallop turned from me as a uniformed policeman approached. We three eyed the No Parking sign for a silent moment.

"Mornin', Father," said the policeman.

"Good morning, Joe. Will you keep an eye on the car for me?"

198

"Sure, Father. I'll watch it." Father Wallop smiled and we turned away.

At the door of the Municipal Building he paused and sighed, then he pulled from the pocket of his suit a folded brown paper sack, a grocery bag. "I wish I could think of some other way to get you inside. Here, put this over your head."

"That's the crowning indignity."

"I'll give you full marks for the pun. But can you think of another way to get you into the room unseen?"

"Well, you could sling me over your shoulder in the good shepherd pose."

"Just put this over your head and pull it well down over the beard."

It was brown, airless, and uncomfortable within the grocery sack. He took my groping hand and led me up the steps. I stumbled along behind him.

"Morning, George," I heard him say and I heard Salter's growl.

"What've you got there, Padre?"

"What does it look like?"

"Looks like a kid with a paper sack on his head."

"That's right. I suppose the juvenile officer is in?"

"I suppose so; aren't you coming to the inquest?"

"Just as soon as I deal with this fellow."

"What *is* the matter with him?"

"Let's just say his face was flushed."

"Do you mean to tell me that you honestly have a kid

there with his head stuck in a chamber pot! Honestly? This I've got to see."

I heard the shuffle of feet and I shifted away from the noise, hoping that I was moving behind the protective bulk of Father Wallop.

"Now, George, I would hardly be fulfilling my trust to the boy's mother if I let you examine him, would I?"

"Yeh, well. . . ." There was a disgruntled quality to his agreement. "Anyway, Father, I'll see you after the inquest? I want to know just how close you are to that Withers guy."

"Just about as close as you are yourself, George." I thought the priest had gone too far there. Perhaps he did, too, for he hurried on the next question. "Where will the inquest be held?"

"In Room D when they get back. Actually, the inquest is already in session. The coroner and the girl's father have gone over to the mortuary to identify the body officially."

The air inside the paper sack was mouldy, damp and too much used already. It seemed full of hairs and damp dust. I scraped my feet impatiently. Instantly my arm was seized and I was hustled away. The priest hissed against my papered ear, "Are you trying to call attention to those crazy shoes of yours?"

"He has seen my heels only in a metaphorical fashion," I said, but the reply was apparently muffled. I was jerked to a standstill.

"Quick, off with the sack. Stuff it in your pocket."

I clawed at the bag. My hair was damp, my face wet with perspiration, my beard crinkly with sweat. The wadded sack, which I stuffed into my bosom, gave me a faintly Amazonian structure. We stood before closed double doors.

"This is Room D. In, quick!" Clearly the priest was acting out mystery-story fantasies. The corridor was empty and quiet and there seemed no need for haste. But he wrenched open the door, propelled me inside and shoved me painfully into a chair against the back wall. It was a pleasantly airy room, with several rows of chairs facing a large, heavy table, behind which was a high-backed swivel chair. A small desk for the official recorder was placed under the windows to the left. We were the only ones in the room.

Father Wallop mopped his brow in a theatrical manner. "What have I done?" he asked the empty chairs.

"You've undone any good that Johnston might have accomplished with my shoulder," I said, rubbing it in a fashion no less theatrical. An observer of dispassionate temperament, if there had been one, might have observed that we were both enjoying the excitement immensely.

"What have I done?" he repeated. "You have no proof at all?"

"None."

"I'll look a fool if nothing comes of your charges."

"Me too."

"But what if you're right? What if you're right? What if Salter and the whole police force is in on this? How can we stop them?"

"You said it yourself. Make a citizen's arrest."

"Of the whole police force! What if they gun me down?"

"Best thing that could happen for Stratford."

He looked at me with some distaste. "In a certain sense, I mean," I added.

"Yes, I hope you do. You mean the blood of martyrs and all that. But what if they shoot you down?"

"The worst thing that could happen for Stratford."

"But only in one sense," he said smugly.

"I'm the only real witness. No, Father, if it comes to gun play you must shield me with your, um, ample body. But let us hope that it won't come to that. And it won't. Obviously, not too many people can be in on the fix. That would mean cutting the profit too many ways."

"How many?"

"Salter, West, and Hairy Dan. Perhaps there is one more. Or two. . . . Will there be many people at the inquest, besides those?"

"Linda's father will be here. I suppose we can count on him, *if* you can produce some evidence. Can you?"

"I don't know, Father. I really don't." I looked about the room, vainly hoping for a clue, an idea, anything. "Where does that door lead?"

"That? That leads to the morgue."

"Why didn't they put Linda's body there?"

"Well, it's not a very nice place. I know, I've seen it."

"Yeh, but is that usually a consideration with the coroner? I mean, doesn't he usually keep bodies that have met with, um, violent ends in his custody until after the inquest?"

"Yes, but I suppose Linda's father exerted some influence in this instance. He must know something about morgues, after all."

202

"Maybe. How many cadavers will the morgue hold?"

"Stratford's not large, you know. Let me think . . . There's just the one box, kind of a sliding tray affair. Yes, that's all, just one. And the table, of course."

"I'm going to look," I said, but even as I spoke he wrenched me back in my seat.

The recurrent pain in my shoulder I attribute not to the inept probings of Doctor Johnston but directly to the hearty wrench that Father Wallop delivered as the door of Room D slammed open and the coroner entered with his retinue. He was an overweight man, in a wrinkled grey suit; black streaks of greasy hair were plastered across his pate. He walked with his belly well forward, as though butting open saloon doors. Behind him trailed Thumbs Brusick, Gnome Tabor, and the two bodyguards all dressed in their customary suits of solemn black. If not a horde, at least a gaggle or a group of witnesses and spectators straggled through the door behind them.

I saw West and Salter, though they seemed to see neither me nor each other. They rapidly seated themselves. A line of unknowns, what might have been the coroner's jury, occupied the first row; behind them sat the Brusick claque, then the spectators, who included in their number both Salter and West. The reporter occupied the side table and uncased his stenography machine.

The coroner seated himself at the high-backed swivel chair and said, "Readjourn." Really he said, "Rejurn." He continued, "The identification has been established by the next of kin." His enunciation was slovenly even by Stratford standards. "Now we establish the manner of decease. Is Doc Frackel here?" A young man in the second row stood up.

"I was on ambulance duty that night and I answered the call, although it came late. The deceased. . . ."

"Now, wait, Frackel. I wan to remine you that most of us poor slobs, elected representatives or not, haven't had the advantages of your splendid high-grade education. Whatever you was planning to say, just forget it and tell us did she or did she not slice her wrists?"

"That's not my position to say, Coroner. I will testify only to the manner of the death. I will not testify as to who did or did not apply the particular. . . ."

"Awright, *Doctor*." The thick venom with which the coroner coated the word "doctor" gave me an insight into the contempt which Doctor Johnston had shown when he spoke of the coroner. "You just tell us in little short words why she died."

"She bled to death."

"And where at were the wounds?"

"On either wrist."

"Either wrist or both wrists? You gotta remember that we never went to college, Doctor."

"Both wrists were cut. The incision in the left wrist was much the deeper and was probably the one that proved fatal."

"That would mean that the deceased was left-handed?"

"It would probably indicate that she was *right*-handed. If it is ascertained that she was a suicide."

Throughout the petty exchange Thumbs sat looking di-

204

rectly ahead. I could not see his hands; my own were trembling.

"I thank you kindly, Doctor. If you want to get back to that ambulance you're excused. Now, Chief of Detectives George Salter?" Salter stood to give his evidence.

"I wasn't the first to the scene. There was some difficulty with the car. . . ."

"Was that when your car was stolen?"

"I don't think that's relevant here. The point is that Father Wallop was there before I was. He should testify, but I don't think he has come in yet."

"Yes I have," said the priest. Every eye in the place turned upon him, then wavered down to focus on me crouched in the seat at his side. "I arrived at the motel a full thirty minutes before George Salter did. The owner of the motel assured me that he had touched nothing. Linda, that is, the deceased, lay on the bed. There was, God rest her soul, a razor blade on the bed within inches of her right hand."

"Well, that seems to be that. I think we can say that this inquest. . . ."

I rose unsteadily to my feet. I still seemed to be the center of interest anyway. Haltingly I made my way down the center aisle. "If it please your honor," I said.

"Don't call me that; I'm not a judge."

I still wasn't sure what my next move would be. I plodded determinedly down the aisle though, each step bringing me closer to Brusick whom I had erst thought of as enemy.

"What shall I call you?"

"Just say, Coroner."

"Well, Coroner, I have something of importance to say regarding this case." I was stumped to know what it was however.

"Well?" The high swivel chair squeaked with the irritable gesture of the coroner.

"Before I reveal . . . what I have to reveal, may I ask that the room be sealed, closed off, locked up?"

I saw his greasy pate swing in the direction of Salter. The coroner waited a moment for a signal. What the signal was I cannot say; my back was to Salter. But the careful, emphatic nod of the coroner was unmistakable.

"Can't clear the room for every crackpot," he said.

"I didn't say *clear*. I said *rock!* I mean *lock*."

"They's fire laws again that, sonny. You just say what you have to say, if it's worth saying. And if not, don't."

I turned toward Thumbs Brusick, but my lurching mode of locomotion made it appear something more in the way of a lunge. Instantly Tabor and Brusick leapt to their feet as their hands slapped to their shoulder holsters. I found myself fairly clutching Tabor by his lapels.

"You want to know who's responsible for Linda?" I shrieked into his ear. "You want to know who hooked Thumbs' daughter? Then, don't let anybody out of this room."

I think everyone in the room was on his feet by then. I was clinging to the Gnome to maintain my balance and that clutching grasp of mine revealed that the Gnome's gesture toward his shoulder holster had been pure instinct. Like a Pavlov dog who salivated when the dinner bell was rung, the

206

Gnome grabbed for a revolver in moments of excitement, whether he wore a holster or not. Which he didn't! The shoulder I pawed at was pudgy with the hint of matted hair beneath the black cotton shirt, but there was no holster under his arm. I turned and clawed at Thumbs Brusick. "You want to know who hooked your daughter?"

Thumbs raised his arms and cracked me across the wrists. It was a good smart blow, the work of a thoroughly competent wrist smacker, but in the brief instant I clutched at his bosom I learned that he, too, was unarmed. At least his instinctive gesture had been to his shoulder and there he carried no weapon. Could I believe that the thugs had disarmed themselves as a courtesy to the coroner? Or wasn't it more likely that they, ex-convicts and parolees and men under the eye of the law, hadn't brought personal weapons across a state line? Of course! They had come without their side arms. That's why they had planned to kill me with a car rather than a gun.

There came now from the deep within me a clear and demanding voice asking simply what in the world I was up to. It was not the voice of my conscience; *that* was a familiar whine to which I had grown hardened. Or at least adept in answering with a neat rationalization. No, this voice was something new. It was neither querulous nor accusing, but simply bell-like. "Are you Hamlet," it asked, "trying to set the world aright? Or do you think that you're some avenging sword of justice? If it's justice you wish to see meted out, you should call a convention of local taxi drivers and deliver yourself into their hands, bound."

Obviously this clear voice had been listening to my conscience. But by that time there was pandemonium without and bedlam within me. Within, there were other voices to be heard. My conscience, having received some attention for the first time in years, began to babble. My weary body complained piteously of hunger, dizziness, and the sickening wrench to my shoulder that Thumbs Brusick's wrist-crack had caused. In the room there was every bit as much commotion. Brusick and Taber were still on their feet; Salter had moved from his chair to challenge my position in front of the coroner's table. The coroner himself was standing, repeating, "Now, now, now, now, now." He sounded the way a starter on the old Model A Fords sounded on cold mornings. "Now, now, now."

"We'll handle this nut," Salter said, reaching for my bad shoulder. "I've a list of charges on him as long as he is."

"Wait a minute," said Brusick, and Salter's hand stopped in mid-reach. They stood eyeing each other across the crown of my head.

If that same dispassionate but perceptive observer who might have looked in on Father Wallop and myself a few minutes before were to look in now, he would be hard put to it to know which of the two who towered over me represented the forces of law and order, so steady was Brusick's glance, so complete was Salter's obedience to the simple, barked command, "wait a minute." I looked up at Brusick, then I twisted my head and looked up at Salter.

If Brusick *were unarmed*, who had fired the shot at me that had hit me? Who had fired the shots at me that had missed me? Could the fact of Brusick's lack of guns account for Salter's present attitude toward him? How *would* an officer of the law act if publicly confronted by a known criminal of unguessed potential who had seen that same public servant commit a criminal act? Would he search his face for a clue to future conduct in the manner that Salter now searched the face of Brusick over the top of my head?

I slid out from beneath the weighty exchange of stares.

"I want to see the body," I said to the coroner and I inclined my head toward the door that Father Wallop had told me led to the morgue.

"Well, you can't sonny. If you wanted to view the remains you should have been here when the session met over to the mortuary. The remains aren't here in the morgue."

"Why?"

"Don't you be flippant. You sound like a college boy to me. Chief of Detectives Salter, if you can handle this maniac the coroner will be pleased. Will you clear the room of him?"

"Wait a minute," barked Brusick once again. He and Salter seemed to have locked gazes as bull antelopes lock antlers. They swayed slightly but neither took eyes from the other's steady gaze. "Go on, speak up," Brusick said to me.

"Chief Salter?" the coroner said plaintively.

"*Go on!*"

"Why isn't the body in the morgue?"

"Because, sonny, the morgue is full up. We already have a cadaver in the morgue. They's only room for one."

"Has the body been there since Saturday?"

"Since Saturday and before that. I don't see what business this is of yours."

"Who is it?"

"What?"

"Whose body have you in the morgue?"

"I don't know. He's a bindle stiff, an unidentified tramp. A nobody who just happened to die in Stratford. I suppose he was transferring from one college to another and was just passing through our town when he died."

"And what did he die of?"

"Exposure and malnutrition and drinking too much canned heat and staying up late at nights studying about eeevolution."

"Who certified his death?"

"I did. It wasn't difficult to tell he was dead, you know."

"Are you a certified physician?"

"No, I'm proud to say I'm not. I'm the coroner, the duly elected and sworn-in coroner."

"I thought only licensed physicians could sign death warrants."

The coroner glanced about the room. It seemed clear to him that the audience was on his side. I was his opponent, Father Wallop didn't count, and the battle between Salter and Brusick seemed to have lifted them onto a plane of their own where they wrestled immaterially for supremacy.

"Sonny, one of the things I've tried to do is cut down the taxpayers' expenses. It might not be quite, quite legal, but in cases as clear as this, with a fellow headed for Potters' Field at public expense, a fellow who just happened to be in our town when he passed on, it seemed foolish to have the additional expenses of a. . . ."

"Did he die last Friday?"

"I don't remember."

210

"Will your records show?"

"Well, I din't attempt to fix the time of the death. They was no autopsy."

"I think he was shot."

"Well, he wasn't. So you can just *stop* thinking it."

"Will you let me examine the body?"

"I will not!"

"Do you mean to sit there and say that you won't let a relative view the body of a deceased member of his family?"

The coroner was shaken. In a gesture that might have been meaningful twenty years before he ran a hand through his hair. The hand came away slick with grease and the slick black strands that had lain across his skull stood cock-a-doodle upright on his head.

"You related to the remains?"

"No man is an island entire of itself; every man is a piece of the continent, a part of the main."

"You say the name is Main?"

"No, Donne."

"Dunne?"

"Done."

"That ain't his name."

"Oh? Did he have identification papers on him?"

"No."

"Well?"

"Well, what? I won't have any more of this tomfiddlery. Chief of Detectives Salter, I wish you would do something else aside from standing up and staring down."

I shared, if not the coroner's exasperation, at least his bewilderment at Salter's continued inactivity. Then with a de-

211

lighted start I realized that I was the only one in the room who suspected that the menacing silent figures of Thumbs Brusick, his thug Tabor and the two black-suited body-guards who stood behind their champion, were all unarmed. But any moment Salter would call their bluff. The four hood-lums stood statuesque, their right hands tucked into their left armpits. What would they do if Salter reached for his gun? None of them could pull out a revolver, I was sure. I hated to think of the state of Tabor's hand when he withdrew it from the dank armpit; but terrible as it might be, it would hardly be weapon enough to oppose Salter's service revolver.

That was it! Service revolver. And, incidentally, it occurred to me that I stood in direct line of Salter's fire. I hopped briskly onto the coroner's table, crossed my legs and asked Thumbs, "Do you carry a service revolver?"

"No."

"But Chief of Detectives Salter does, doesn't he?" I turned on the table to lean menacingly at the coroner. "And that was the gun that he used to kill Jim Downey. Because Jim Downey discovered that it was Salter who was supporting and protecting the dope peddlers, right? Right! And he told you to keep Jim Downey's body in the morgue until the excitement died down and then you could bury the body quietly in Potters' Field. At public expense. And Downey's body has been in your vile morgue since Friday; that's why Linda was taken to a mortuary. Linda Brusick was so ashamed when Jim Downey found out about her addiction that she tried to quit. She tried to cold-turkey herself—locked herself in a motel room until she could shake the monkey off

212

her back. Only it was too much for her. But Salter would have killed her anyway, wouldn't you?" I swung back from the cowed and trembling coroner.

"I do what I'm told," he was saying. "I don't have an education. This is the only job I have. I do what they tell me to do."

But Salter's gun was out. The Chicago backfield made no move. He had cleanly called their bluff.

"You fakers, you're all four unarmed." The service revolver swung menacingly from them to me and back to the black-clad four. Salter walked backward in the direction of the door. "Don't move. Don't breathe. Don't think." He backed rapidly away.

From the rear of the room Father Wallop moved to meet him.

"All right, George, if he's wrong in his accusations you can sue him."

Salter whirled. "Get out of my way. Padre."

Father Wallop stepped forward. One step, then another. "Come on, George. You're not a priest-killer. Give me the gun."

"Get out of my way!" His minute brow wrinkled violently. For a moment priest and decadent detective stood facing each other in the aisle. "Damn it!" screamed Salter and he hurled his revolver at the priest's head. Father Wallop ducked neatly and the Chicago wing backs fell upon Salter. The struggle was brief, over before it had begun really because Salter had capitulated when he threw the gun.

Above the turmoil I saw a sudden movement toward the

door in the rear. Edward West was easing his way out of the room.

"There's the pusher," I cried. I admit with shame (tinged with smugness) that I felt joy when I saw Gnome Tabor deliver an overhand blow to the back of West's head. West fell like an ox, as Virgil would have said.

"Who else?" shouted Brusick. "Who else?" He shook Salter with terrible violence. "Who else? I kill you!"

"Only Dan," the shaken, battered, kicked Salter gasped.

The bodyguards trotted smartly from the room in search of Dan. I felt confident that he would be taken. People in Chicago whom I knew personally through my poolroom association would have refused to credit the evidence of their senses during the past few minutes if they had been there. The sight of Thumbs Brusick arresting an officer of the law was staggering to the hoariest imagination. But there he stood, towering in his new-found virtue, shaking Salter as a terrier might shake an old rag. Slowly, almost surreptitiously, other law officers began infiltrating the room, first a sheriff, then several uniformed policemen. One of them had clearly abandoned his post at Father Wallop's auto.

I found myself pumping Father Wallop's hand while I shouted into the din, "I knew the dope peddlers weren't worried about Linda Brusick. Their time schedule, you know. The heat going off and on. Jim Downey's death was the only other event remarkable in this town. He must have seen something wrong with her, in class probably. Maybe she confessed to him. And then he marched righteously into Salter's office to report the existence of narcotics in Stratford.

214

Salter had to silence him and he saw no other way but to kill poor old Downey."

"God rest his soul. When did you first suspect Salter?"

"During my first week working in that poolroom in Chicago. If the police can know as much about crime as they do in a city that size, the police ought to know everything about the underworld in Stratford. I really didn't think he had killed Downey until I realized that Salter and not Brusick had shot me."

"It's a wonder."

"Listen, Father, will you call Sister Mary Ransom at the college and tell her that I'll be there for my classes tomorrow. Tell her that I'll lecture on Elizabeth Barrett Browning and 'Sonnets from the Congo.'"

"I'm sure that they'll be proud to have you on the faculty."

"Maybe, but if you could, imply that I have a verbal contract and that I'll sue if they *don't* take me on. Oh, and while you're at it, will you call the Yellow Cab and ask them if they want vengeance or ten dollars?"

"What ten dollars?"

"The ten I put into your collection last Sunday. Could I have it now?"

"I'll let you make restitution in person," he said, although that wasn't exactly what I had in mind. "In fact, I'll drive you to the cab company office."

As we drove along I had a sudden vision of myself babysitting for Bartie Barstairs and Mary. They would provide me with lists of emergency instructions and lists of emergency telephone numbers. Before they left for their festive

215

evening at the neighborhood movie and after their return, they would offer me sly but eager encouragements to save, shave, and marry. They would try to mate me with some good and nearly-young parish maiden with a horsey face.

"What's horsey-face's name?" I asked Father Wallop as he twisted his car from the No Parking Zone and eased it through a yellow light. "Shirley," he answered promptly, and immediately said, "I mean, what did you say? I mean, I didn't hear you surely." He was quick-witted, but the intelligence had leaked. The Barstairs were not the only ones plotting the imminent reformation of poor, dear, old, shot-up Red Withers.

"Hey, Father, why not take me to the train station. I'm sure to find one of my dupes there. You can see me eat humble pie and all that with your ten dollars."

"Well, the main office is just down the block."

"Come on, give the old station a try. It would be good for me to — you know?"

"There probably won't be any cabs there."

"I thought I just heard a train whistle. Did you?"

"That must have been the express to the West Coast."

"Oh, I'd hate to be locked in a jake all the way to Hollywood." I don't think he heard me; anyway he ignored me.

"That might be the New York Special though; it's due about this time."

"Well, listen, all the cabs on duty will probably be at the station. Let's swing down and see."

He fished a ten dollar bill from his pocket and thrust it somewhat ungraciously into my hand. "Will this be enough?"

"Well, Father, almost." I felt another bill and spoke even before I dared to see what denomination it was. "Thank you, Father, thank you. And . . ." I shrugged in a boyish, winning way as Father Wallop turned into the station parking lot. He maneuvered past No Entry signs, around No Turn signs, and against One Way signs to align himself as the last car in the rank of taxi cabs. There were four cabs in front of him and such was the neatness of his driving, only a curbing and embankment behind him. We arrived almost simultaneously with the train whose whistle we had heard.

I screwed about in the front seat to view the large, the kindly and brave profile of the dear old bear Father Wallop. "You know, Salter told me that this town was his, but it isn't. It's yours."

"Well, love conquers where hate fails. *Amor vincit omnia.*"

"Hey, Father, that's a line from Chaucer!"

"I know."

"You ought to teach a course at Saint Felicitas sometime."

"Yes, well, I do think about it off and on. It would be fun. I mean, an awful lot of work and all that . . ."

But he had, of course, sealed his fate. Mine too. He had as good as sealed me into the jakes. Baby-sitting, indeed; and that horsey-faced maiden.

"Watch now," I said, "I'll just go pay the debt to society or the cab company or whatever." I slipped from his car and trotted briskly (alertly!) forward. In the cab just in front of Father Wallop's auto sat the cabbie who had driven me from the station to Father Wallop's church only the Sunday before. I averted my face and trotted smartly on. The next cab contained the driver who had driven me from the college to the police station in the dark of the night. The next cab in line was the taxi that had first borne me to the vicinity of Bartie Barstairs' home. I fairly raced past that one with averted face and beard. The lead taxi proved unfamiliar. I chanced one, quick backward glance at Father Wallop. He grinned reassurance.

"Listen," I said, thrusting my head into the open window. "Do you know the Padre?"

"Fodder Wallop?"

"Him. Well, his car is stuck in the rear of the cab rank and he has an emergency call."

"I'll swing the old cab around and give him a push."

"You can't do that." (I heard the train give a peremptory whistle.) "He's backed against the embankment."

"Just like the Padre. Well, I got three guys behind me, lucky for him. We'll all give him a push." He hopped out of his cab as I swung about on my makeshift heels and headed toward the pausing train. It was a flag-stop (well, it was Providence was what it was) and the conductor had not locked the jakes. I did, of course. I locked it behind me. The last glimpse I had of Stratford was the incredulous face of Father Wallop, glimpsed through the narrow window, as four strange cabbies moved in upon him intent upon pushing his car about.